'You're a ve
mega chip o

'And you think you might be ...
Sasha said with cynicism.

'I'm going to try...'

Richard's hand reached up and slid beneath her
shirt, and very slowly he brushed the back of
his hand across her breasts. His touch was
temptation, his words a sexual spur...

'I'm going to make love to you so long and
intensely that "inhibition" is a word you'll soon
forget.'

Natalie Fox was born and brought up in London and has a daughter, two sons and two grandchildren. Her husband, Ian, is a retired advertising executive, and they now live in a tiny Welsh village. Natalie is passionate about her cats—two strays brought back from Spain where she lived for five years—and equally passionate about gardening and writing romance. Natalie says she took up writing because she absolutely *hates* going out to work!

Recent titles by the same author:

PROMISE OF PASSION

PASSION WITH INTENT

BY
NATALIE FOX

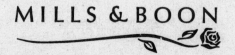

MILLS & BOON

*MILLS & BOON and the Rose Device
are trademarks of the publisher.
Harlequin Mills & Boon Limited,
Eton House, 18-24 Paradise Road, Richmond, Surrey TW9 1SR*

© Natalie Fox 1996

ISBN 0 263 14650 2

*Set in Times Roman 10 on 12 pt.
07-9602-53922 C1*

Made and printed in Great Britain

CHAPTER ONE

SASHA was swinging perilously from the veranda, gathering her breakfast, when she heard three toots from the Chinese trader boat as it chugged slowly and laboriously towards the island *en route* to the bigger island of Kula, a couple of nautical miles along this stretch of the Solomons.

With a whoop that summoned Ruth from the wooden bungalow they shared she swung her bare legs over the veranda, plopped the pawpaw into Ruth's arms and leapt down the wooden steps to the beach and the canoe.

'Have you got the new generator, Ko-chi?' she shouted over the chug of his ancient engines as she paddled furiously out to the trader.

With a wide grin Ko-chi gave her the thumbs up and slowed the engines enough for Sasha to come alongside.

The coral reef around the tiny island made landing for any sort of seacraft other than the narrow pirogues the islanders used impossible. Ko-chi was coming as close as he could and the rest was up to Sasha.

Skilfully she paddled the canoe till it was broadside to the old rust-bucket. Reaching for the rickety ladder, she secured the canoe and scrambled up the rungs. A hand came down to assist her up the last few rungs and swing her over the side of the trader.

She was standing in front of a tall, dark stranger before she knew it, her hand and lower arm tingling from the powerful contact with a man she didn't know, her heart thudding dangerously—and not from the exertion of climbing aboard. The stranger was stunningly impressive.

'Oh,' she breathed, smoothing her flimsy vest-top down over crumpled khaki shorts, feeling maddeningly self-conscious as she compared her scruffy attire with the way he was dressed—in tropical whites.

Ko-chi sometimes took passengers on his island-hopping trader and this man obviously wasn't a deckhand. He said nothing by way of introduction, as if she was nothing to do with him, but it didn't stop him giving her the once-over, and even a twice-over.

Sasha burned under his blatant perusal of her, felt colour rise up to her throat. Not to be put out, though, she did likewise, running her eyes effectively up and down him to cover the shock of the impact he had made on her senses.

He had everything Ruth would drop dead for, Sasha mused—height, breadth, and wealth, by the look of the cut of his clothes and the chunky gold watch on his left wrist. Endowed with good looks enhanced by a dark tan and fascinating grey eyes that had the power to melt bones, he was certainly a cut above anything the islands had seen for a long time.

Sasha's bones weren't melting, though, she decided. She had expected Ko-chi to haul her aboard and was just shocked that a stranger had appeared out of nowhere. That was why her heart was racing. She was immune to men and had been for two years now.

The lingering eye contact between them was suddenly broken by Ko-chi dragging several baskets across the deck to her.

'Supplies now and you come Kula for generator,' he told her. 'You tip pirogue if you take it now.'

'You're right, Ko-chi. Thanks. I'll pay you when I come into Kula later.'

She bent down to haul one of the baskets over the side, half expecting the stranger to assist her, but when she looked back he had gone. Ko-chi lowered the basket, tied up with reed rope, into the canoe for her while Sasha gazed around the cargo-laden deck for another sight of the stranger, but she saw no one but Ko-chi's boys, smoking by a pile of chicken crates.

'Who's your passenger?' Sasha asked as the last basket went over the side and plopped into the canoe below.

Ruth would kill her if she didn't find out. For herself she was more interested in why he was here. Two years and she still suffered stabs of fear when a stranger came to the islands, always suspecting that her past was catching up with her.

Ko-chi shrugged his bony old shoulders. 'Tourist maybe.' He rubbed his thumb across his fingers in a gesture suggesting money. 'Plenty this,' he laughed. 'I ask no questions. The bambo with him...' he made another gesture, screwing his gnarled forefinger into the side of his temple '...she trouble.'

'Bimbo, you mean,' Sasha laughed.

'Yeah, that,' grinned the Chinaman.

Still laughing, Sasha swung herself over the side, down the ladder and into the canoe. She untied and picked up the paddle and used it to push herself away from the trader.

'See you later at Kula,' she shouted as she paddled away. She sensed Ko-chi's passenger watching her as she skimmed through the water, and in a sudden flash of rebelliousness she looked back to make sure. He was indeed watching her through narrowed eyes, quite determinedly, too. With his elbows on the rail of the trader he was watching her every movement. The nerve, she fumed, looking at me like that and with a 'bambo' in tow!

'So who was that? He looked amazing. Come on, who is he? Where is he going and does he want a wife?' were the questions that bubbled from Ruth's lips as soon as Sasha leapt ashore. Ruth had obviously been watching it all. Together they hauled the canoe clear of the surf.

Sasha took one last look at the stranger as the trader chugged further and further away towards Kula. He was still leaning on the rail, still looking in her direction, so totally out of place on Ko-chi's battered boat that Sasha frowned with concern as she looked down at her arm where he had hauled her aboard.

She shivered slightly. She had half expected to see some sort of brand mark where he had touched her. The mark of the devil . . .

'Sasha?'

She jumped, looked at Ruth and grinned. 'You might stand more of a chance as a mistress,' Sasha told her cryptically, remembering that long sexual perusal of her when she had stood before him on the deck.

'I'll go for that,' Ruth said eagerly. 'So who is he—a tourist?'

'Probably,' Sasha murmured, though she doubted it. Tourists came in gleaming cruise-ships, not Chinese traders, and tourists wore garish shorts and T-shirts. That man was dressed in tropical whites and appeared to be a very out-of-place businessman. He worried her. They saw few businessmen on these islands.

She shrugged the feeling away, refusing to let it get to her, but she couldn't prevent a little crumb of doubt lingering on. Strangers bothered her, unsettled her—but no, two years was a long time.

'You're not even curious, are you?' Ruth grumbled as they struggled up the beach with the baskets of supplies.

'Nope, not in the least,' Sasha told her with conviction, but her senses weren't quite so convinced. He was an attractive man and she had allowed herself to acknowledge it, but not for the world would she let on to Ruth. Ruth would make a meal of it and expect seconds.

'Come with me to Honiara,' Ruth suggested over breakfast on the veranda, after they had unpacked the supplies which Sasha had ordered to tide her over till Ruth came back. 'You're due some leave too. We'll have a ball—hunting men and sharing our spoils.'

Sasha grinned at her suggestion and sidestepped the last part of it. 'We can't both take leave at the same time,' she said sensibly. 'Happy hunting in Honiara. You're on your own, Ruth.'

In a way she wished she were a bit more like Ruth— honestly open about her needs where men were concerned. Two years' celibacy in Ruth's eyes was a term worse than death, and she had told Sasha so when, in a weak moment, Sasha had admitted that she'd had no brush with the opposite sex in the time she'd been on the islands. She'd instantly regretted her words and had added, in a feeble attempt to cover herself, that running the clinic in Kula was all the satisfaction she needed.

The truth she'd held back. To Sasha men were taboo, or *tambu*, as the islanders said. Geoff had betrayed her so badly that she still couldn't think back on her past with him without a deep shudder running through her.

Her discovery on the day before their society wedding in Auckland had so horrified her that she had fled and in doing so had opened up such a painful riot of hatred and scorn against her that to return with any degree of honour was impossible. Geoff had done his worst in revenge and Sasha had built a new life for herself, far away from the past.

'Hurry up, Ruth,' Sasha urged. She was taking Ruth over to Kula on the first stage of her trip to Honiara, the capital of the islands. She took her oilskin cape down from the hook on the porch and threw it on hurriedly. The sky was looking mutinous and she wanted to drop Ruth off and pick up her generator before the rain started.

Ruth staggered out onto the porch with enough gear packed for a year's stay, let alone a month. That would slow down their progress, Sasha thought ruefully as she helped stow the stuff in the bottom of the fibreglass canoe.

'What a way to live,' Ruth grumbled as she huddled into her waterproofs and stepped into the bobbing craft. 'I could be theatre sister in any hospital I chose instead of in this God-forsaken place.'

'You love it,' Sasha laughed, knowing she did. It was the challenge—the same challenge that had gripped Sasha when she had come to the islands, the challenge and the deep personal satisfaction that came from helping people. Though Sasha wasn't on the medical team, she ran the administration side of the clinic and all the other offshoots of the practice; her work was equally important and rewarding.

It was a far cry from her pampered life in New Zealand and to some it would seem that she had done it as some sort of penance, seeking redemption for what she had *apparently* done to Geoff.

Geoff's revenge had taken the form of blackening her name and morals after she had left and he'd convinced everyone that she had been the wrongdoer. He'd done the job so convincingly that even her own family had been bemused by his allegations. She had done nothing to convince them otherwise; the whole affair had been sordid enough without her retaliating and making matters worse.

She only had contact with her father now; her stepmother had long since disowned her, furious that the marriage plans for her stepdaughter had been thwarted. Her father wrote twice a year, begging her to return, saying that people would forgive and forget. She had nothing to be forgiven for but the truth from her wouldn't be believed. Geoff's family were too powerful and they would have seen that their son came out of the whole mess squeaky-clean.

Talk was impossible on the pirogue. The outboard engine was noisy and the spray from the sea a chilling dampener to conversation. Sasha concentrated hard on negotiating the canoe through the coral reef and then onward to open water and Kula, which rose threateningly out of the green sea, its forest peaks drenched in rain and mist.

The stranger would be long gone now, she hoped, but there was that crumb of interest still hanging around, only out of curiosity, though. Half-decent-looking strangers were few and far between on the islands.

Sasha dropped Ruth off at the first pier at Kula where her connecting boat, a far more civilised motor cruiser, was awaiting to take her to the primitive airstrip on the far side of the island where she would pick up a flight to Honiara.

They were all used to this island-hopping—no choice, really—and took it in their stride. The rain too. It had started gently now, but it would soon work its way up to a fury. With any luck she would be back before it gained too much momentum.

'I'll miss you,' Ruth groaned as she gave Sasha a hug. 'I wish you were coming with me. I hate to think of you alone on that island, backwards and forwards to the clinic every other day, working your fingers to the bone, and no men in your—'

'Shut up,' Sasha laughed. 'You know I love it—peace and quiet without you bending my ear every five minutes. Now don't forget that list I gave you.'

'Make-up, perfumes, silk underwear—'

'Some chance,' Sasha chortled.

'Yeah, some chance,' Ruth grinned ruefully as she threw her bags onto the deck of the waiting cruiser and eased out of her waterproofs to fling them into the bottom of the canoe. Such luxuries as she had listed were not only scarce in this corner of the world but maddeningly expensive if you did happen to find them.

Sasha waved goodbye and then scrambled back into the canoe and whisked along to the end pier where Ko-chi's trader was moored. Already a bustling crowd was gathered in the rain to see the goods he'd brought this trip—no luxuries, just things that were necessary to make life a little easier on the sometimes harsh islands.

Sasha tied up the canoe and, shaking the rain from her dark hair, scrambled up the wooden steps to the deck of the rickety pier.

Her head came up as she heard the commotion coming from beside the wooden shed that served as the harbour master's office.

'Barbarians, all of them!' a woman was shrieking. 'I'm soaked to the skin and no one seems to care—'

'Everyone is soaked to the skin,' came the travel-weary reply. 'Stay where you are while I get things organised.'

The stranger from the trader stepped out from under the overhanging reeded roof of the shed, looked around him as if looking for someone official, and then spotted Sasha. She was standing watching the scene with a mixture of disgust and amusement. He headed towards her.

Barbarians indeed, Sasha fumed inwardly. The Melanesians and Polynesians were kind and hospitable people and if that woman took the time to be patient with them they'd give her all their worldly goods. Not that she would have any use for them. She was dressed as if for a garden party and was holding a frivolous parasol over her head, totally useless against the downpour.

Sasha might have felt sorry for her if it hadn't been for the remark about the islanders and what she was doing now—hurling invectives as stinging as sharp pebbles at a small boy who was trying to sell her a necklace of pink shells. Sasha's hackles had well and truly risen by the time the stranger from the trader reached her.

'There should be a car to pick us up but there has obviously been a breakdown in communication,' he barked as if it were all her doing.

His temper was obviously on a very taut, short lead, and Sasha objected to being on the dog-collar end of it when she thought that awful parasol woman deserved it more. She said nothing, but simply stared at him insolently as if she couldn't understand what all the fuss was about.

She was delighted to see that his designer whites hadn't held up very well during the tropical downfall. His shirt was saturated and looked like a crumpled white paper bag; his dark hair was soaked and flattened to his forehead; his eyes were flaming with impatience, and yet for all of that he still had an air of authority about him.

'I have a lady-friend with me,' he told her hurriedly, 'and she doesn't like hanging around in hell-holes getting wet, so if— '

Sasha spoke at last. 'So if she doesn't want her head shrunk and hung on one of the *barbarians*' belts she'd better buzz off!'

She turned away, angry at that 'bambo's' attitude. So it was raining and she was wet; what the devil was she doing here in the Solomons, then?

Her arm was suddenly wrenched at and she was swung round to face his wrath. 'Well, if I thought they still did that here I'd offer *all* women up on a silver platter. Now will you please stop fooling around and organise a car for us? You obviously know your way around here and we don't.'

Rain poured down from his face and dripped off his chin and had she been confronted with anyone else in such a state her heart would have ached for them. Her heart *was* aching, as it happened, but it wasn't with sympathy. Her green eyes widened in wonderment at the realisation that her heart was playing up again. Arrogant as he was, demanding as he was, he was nevertheless a powerfully attractive man—but not magnetic enough to have her grovelling at his feet.

'The custom might gain favour again—in the not too distant future if I have a hand in it,' she added meaningfully. 'Misogynists would be the first on my belt!'

His grip on her eased, only slightly but enough for Sasha to believe that he might be sorry for his cavalier attitude. He didn't apologise, though.

'It's been a long haul here,' he said wearily and slightly indulgently, as if talking to someone not quite all there, 'and we're tired, hot, very wet and rather short-tempered. I need a car, and quick. Enjoyable as all this pleasant exchange between us is—' sarcasm now '—I'd rather take a rain check on it.'

'Oh, very witty,' Sasha scathed, pulling her arm away from his hold. She was about to walk away when an idea came to her. She faced him, her dripping chin raised defiantly. 'I might be able to help,' she said sweetly. She held out her hand. And why not? The clinic needed every cent it could get its hands on and why shouldn't she get something for her services?

The stranger stared at her in astonishment—obviously weighing up how much the comfort of his lady-friend was worth, Sasha mused as she waited. At last, in a huff, he plunged his hand into his trouser pocket and stuffed a handful of dollars into her palm. *Obviously* she was *very* precious to him, she thought as she eyed the mound of notes.

Sasha lifted her oilskin to push the money into her shorts pocket. The stranger's eyes were riveted on her bare brown legs and she felt the heat and quickly spurned it as she let the oilskin drop to cover their nakedness.

'Thank you,' she murmured, and added thornily, 'For the money, not the perusal. Wait there and I'll organise a car for you.'

'And not before time,' he ground out arrogantly, and then added as she swept past him, 'Aren't you interested in where we're going?'

'There's only one place you can be going,' she told him airily as she hurried on without looking back at him.

Sasha went into the reed-roofed shed that served as a harbour office, called the only hotel on the island and spoke in pidgin, organising a car to come down to the pier to pick them up. Then she went outside, told them a car was on the way, bid them good day and hurried off, just catching the protestations of the very wet, irate lady as she shook out her ruined parasol.

'Who the bloody hell does she think she is?'

Charming, Sasha thought as she hurried over to Ko-chi and his boat.

Two of the islanders were loading her precious generator into the canoe when Todd Arnold pushed his way through the throng of people on the quayside to get to her. Todd was one of the team of doctors in the practice, and specialised in eye surgery. His wife, Tina, had given birth to their first child only two weeks ago.

'You haven't forgotten John Harvey's party tonight, have you, Sasha?'

She swung round to him, her face blank, so deep in speculation about the stranger that she wouldn't have been able to quote her date of birth at that moment.

Her hand came up to her wet forehead as she remembered.

''Struth, yes, I had, actually. Oh, hell, do I have to come? I've a million things to do.'

She glanced up at the sky, which was as leaden as her heart at the thought of the social gathering tonight at Harvey's villa. Such occasions were always a sharp reminder of her previous life in New Zealand—a lot of socialites gathering to bitch about lesser mortals. Not that socialites were thick on the ground on this particular group of islands but there were sometimes visitors in yachts and the people that ran businesses on the islands.

'Yes, you do have to come,' Todd insisted, with a grin. 'John's grants to the hospital and clinics are important to us. We can't afford to offend him.'

Sasha sighed in resignation. 'Yes, I know.'

Damn, she'd have to stay overnight. She had a room at the hospital complex—in a block with the other hospital staff—and usually spent three or four nights there a week anyway when she was working, but she had a couple of days off and always spent her free time on the tiny island of Suya. It was more like a home than the hospital block and she valued her independence.

Ruth had joined her a year ago, wanting respite on her days off away from the operating theatre, and the island suited her too, though she didn't often admit it.

Sasha shrugged. 'No point in going home now, then, in this weather,' she told Todd. 'I'll make arrangements to have this stowed till tomorrow, then I'll go along to see Tina and the baby.'

'She'll be glad to see you. She loves showing the baby off. By the way, she won't be coming tonight so I'll pick you up later and we'll go together. OK?'

'Fine,' she agreed, musing that a couple of years back she wouldn't have taken that suggestion as easily as now. But she'd grown up since then. Of course affairs happened if you wanted them to, but Sasha didn't and she'd soon learnt that if you gave out the right signals a lot of embarrassment could be avoided.

Men didn't make passes at her, single or married. She gave off negative impulses before they even thought of it—the safety barrier she had slammed up after Geoff.

By nightfall the rain had ceased but the weather was decidedly steamy, indeed so hot and humid that breathing was an effort, so the thought of Harvey's air-conditioned palace held more appeal for Sasha than it had that morning.

'Usual crowd, I suppose,' she commented drily as they entered the open doors of the villa where John was greeting guests.

'Do I detect a hint of cynicism?' Todd asked, taking her elbow and guiding her into the reception room, which was the size of a small ballroom and delightfully cool.

'Not really, but these dos are always a bit samey.'

'We have to suffer them, though—'

'Yes, for the sake of the hospital,' Sasha laughed.

While Todd went for drinks she stood by a group of floor-standing plants, gazing out over the veranda and reflecting that her laughter had sounded rather hollow to her own ears.

Had there been a hint of cynicism in her comment? She had never particularly enjoyed these gatherings and

tonight wouldn't be any different she supposed. But tonight she did feel different—no, *today* she felt different,
and why she didn't know. Maybe she was overtired;
maybe she should have taken her leave with
Ruth; maybe—

'Miraculous transformation,' a voice came from beside
her. 'I'd never have recognised you but for the legs.'

Sasha swung around, her thick mane of dark brown
hair swishing across her cheeks. An unaccustomed rush
of blood coloured her face as she recognised the stranger.
Then her eyes went down to her dress as if she had forgotten what she was wearing—pearl-grey silk with a
sarong-style skirt, with the wrap-over part showing a
good deal of golden leg! She flicked at the fine fabric
and it fell back into place.

'You got to the hotel all right, then?' were the first
words that came to her lips. Obviously he had; he looked
a far cry from the harassed, wet stranger who had arrogantly demanded her help on the pier this morning.
His jet-coloured hair was dry now, beautifully cut and
blow-dried, and he wore a lightweight white suit. He was
easily the best-looking, sharpest-dressed, smoothest-
tongued creep in the whole place.

'Yes, unfortunately.' He clipped the words as if the
reminder was a pain.

Sasha shrugged. 'Well, it isn't the Savoy and you're
not the Prince of Wales and it's all there is. Whatever
did you expect on a small tropical island like this?'

'I expected that after I'd crossed your palm with silver
you would arrange a car to take us to our destination,
not some fly-blown, third-rate cowshed on stilts.' He
smiled thinly as Sasha raised her chin, ready to defend
the tiny hotel, her mouth already forming words.

Henrietta's words, not mine,' he added glibly before she could give birth to any of hers. 'My lady-friend.'

'Endorsed by you, no doubt,' she said spikily. 'Well, I'm sorry the place didn't come up to your expectations, but then I suppose the Savoy wouldn't come up to your expectations either. There is no pleasing some people.'

'No, indeed,' he appeared to agree. 'The place certainly didn't come up to expectations as it wasn't where we were going. Here was where we were headed.'

Sasha parted her full lips in surprise. She'd naturally assumed that they were going to stay at the hotel. She felt herself colouring. 'Oh—oh, I'm sorry...'

Their eyes locked, the granite-grey of his softened only by a hint of humour. 'Oh, you will be, I promise you, when Henrietta lashes her tongue around you. She doesn't like to be messed around, you see.'

Recovered now, Sasha fielded that threat with drawling sarcasm. 'Really? She's come to the wrong place, then. The islanders don't intentionally mess visitors around but the lifestyle here is very laid-back and if you don't recognise it and accept it you'll be in for a rough ride. I wish you a pleasant stay.'

She went to walk away but the stranger was having none of it. He caught her arm and gently but firmly turned her to face him. His touch stiffened her. His expression was one of scathing mockery.

'You're a feisty little brat, aren't you?'

Sasha widened her eyes in false surprise and wrenched her elbow away from him. 'Am I expected to agree with that?'

'I spoke rhetorically.'

'It was an insult none the less.'

'Not a serious one. You'd have known if there was malice behind it.'

'Not knowing you, I'm not able to judge that,' she countered, holding those deep grey eyes defiantly.

'Perhaps we ought to put that to rights, then, and get to know each other better.'

He smiled then, engagingly, and her heart thudded so unexpectedly that she wondered what was happening to her. He was flirting with her, and after their verbal sparring of this morning she'd thought that her signals couldn't have been clearer.

'Are you here in connection with the island hospital?' she asked tightly.

'Nope,' he answered.

Sasha smiled sweetly. 'In that case I see no point in our getting to know each other better. You're obviously *en route* elsewhere—'

'We'll be here for a month or more, depending, but that is irrelevant. At this moment we are enjoying a very pleasant social gathering and, seeing as you are the most beautiful woman in the room, I'd like to get to know you more intimately.'

Sasha's eyes widened even more. Some smooth talker, this one, she thought.

'Aren't you forgetting Henrietta the Hun?' she said deliberately caustically. 'The "we" of your conversation.'

'I am indeed,' he said noncommittally, glancing around the room as if seeking her out.

As his eyes settled on Todd, deeply engrossed in conversation with some of the other guests, Sasha realised that he hadn't been looking for the Hun at all. He nodded towards Todd. He must have seen them coming in together.

'Your lover?'

'A friend,' Sasha said, tight-lipped, resisting the urge to ask what business it was of his anyway, considering that to be too predictable.

'Close or getting that way?' His eyes penetrated her so deeply that she felt a chill of apprehension.

'He's a married man,' Sasha told him, her chin going up defensively.

He didn't have to say a word; it was all there in the questioning eye contact. For the first time in a long while it was brought home to her just what sort of a lifestyle she had fled from and why. This stranger was making assumptions that were so damned obvious. She wasn't even going to lower herself by trying to explain.

She began to turn away but once again his grip on her halted her.

'I've offended you.'

Her eyes narrowed. 'Not at all. You offend yourself, not me. You appear to be a well-educated, worldly man and yet you think the thoughts of a *much* lesser man.'

'You don't know what I was thinking.' His eyes were suddenly hard as if *she* had offended *him*.

'Ah, but I do,' she breathed softly, and held his eyes because no one cowed her these days.

'I think it a natural supposition to make—beautiful woman accompanied to a party by a married man. I'd imagine passions run high in this tropical world.'

The rat, Sasha inwardly seethed; the patronising heel!

'Oh, they do,' she agreed. 'So high that murder is within the scope of the most timid of us,' she told him calmly but meaningfully. She wasn't going to show him just how deeply he irritated her.

He smiled thinly. 'Timid you certainly are not.'

'So beware,' she warned him, a brow raised to emphasise the warning. 'Now if you'll excuse me—'

'Certainly not,' he drawled in a teasing tone. 'I'm beginning to think life would be worthless without you.'

She gazed at the sudden humour in his eyes. A man you could never trust to be serious, she mused, or never be able to take seriously, which was subtly different. Whatever, not the sort of man to trust with your emotions.

She realised that her emotions were scarily close to the surface of her thoughts. Yes, and why not? He angered her; that was the emotion crawling over her skin. Regrettably she couldn't hold it back any longer.

Eyes glittering, she said, 'I'd say your life was quite worthless without any help from me. I do realise that the islands can be a cultural shock to some, but anyone with an ounce of reasonableness can come to terms with it.

'So far, you and your friend have insulted the natives, thrown scorn on the local hotel that always does its best with its limited resources, and dragged my morality through the filthy back passages of your mind. I don't even find you amusing, Mr Whatever-your-name-is, and my life would certainly not be worthless if I never saw you again. Have you got the message? Or is your skin so thick—?'

'Ah, darlings,' John Harvey enthused theatrically, suddenly at their side and taking Sasha completely unawares—so much so that she took an involuntary step back and felt a hot rush of colour surge into her cheeks. As quick as a flash-fire the thought came to her that she had been in the throes of deeply insulting the stranger, and the stranger was John's guest, and John Harvey wasn't a man to upset. She hoped that he hadn't over-heard a word of the conversation.

'I see you've already met, so no need for introduc-tions. But you haven't met Henrietta yet.' He turned and beckoned the Hun across to his side. She came im-mediately, lithe and beautiful and expensively dressed, her lovely blue eyes shimmering for only one person in the group—the stranger.

'This is my lovely niece, Henrietta,' he announced proudly to Sasha. 'Her first visit to the Solomons—'

'And probably my last,' Henrietta said abrasively, her eyes settling on Sasha and recognising her from the quayside.

'Come, my dear,' laughed John, giving her a playful hug. 'You got off to a bad start but—'

'We got off to a bad start because of some infantile prank by this young lady,' she blurted out scathingly, her eyes icy with contempt.

Sasha wondered at the look and came to the con-clusion that it was driven not by this morning's mis-understandings but by jealousy. So far at this party the stranger had been giving Sasha more attention than was good for him, unasked for as it was.

Suddenly she felt a reassuring hand cupping her elbow from behind.

'It wasn't a prank, Henrietta, but a simple misunder-standing,' the stranger said quietly.

His defence Sasha didn't need, but under the icy glare of the brutal Henrietta she had to admit that his support was welcome.

'I'm sorry if I misdirected you,' Sasha said, hoping her apology would be accepted. She could do without the wrath of John Harvey's niece. 'I naturally assumed you were staying at the hotel. I didn't know—'

'You didn't wait to find out,' Henrietta bit out, 'and you had the audacity to demand money for the pleasure of dumping us at some atrociously poor excuse for a hotel!'

Sasha felt her colour deepen from crimson to burgundy. She opened her mouth to protest but nothing came out.

'It appears the whole island is flushed with beggars, Uncle John; I don't know how—'

'That is an insult to the islanders!' Sasha protested, finding her voice. 'No one begs here!'

'You did!'

'I offered a reward for Sasha's services,' the stranger interjected immediately.

'And I took it for the hospital,' Sasha said quickly, anticipating a full-blown row and fielding it for the sake of the hospital and her host, John. 'I'm sorry if I gave the impression of begging but...' Her voice trailed off. She suddenly realised that the stranger had said her name and she could have sworn that no one had mentioned it yet. No, no one had. So how...? Her heart raced in panic. He knew her name!

'Your apology is accepted, Sasha, dear,' John said warmly. 'Henrietta has a lot to learn about our ways so please don't be offended by her remarks. She's had a simply dreadful time getting here and perhaps this evening wasn't such a good idea for her and...'

Sasha didn't hear much more. She had reasoned her panic away with cold common sense. The stranger didn't know her; how could he? Now, in total fascination, she was watching Henrietta give the stranger the most poisonous of looks. The stranger's support for the 'beggar' had maddened her so much that she was throwing daggers of fury at him. The stranger seemed completely unaware. Sasha wondered at their relationship, if there was one. But they were here together, had arrived together...

'Richard and Henrietta will be here for about a month and I'm sure you'll get ample chance to...'

Sasha tuned back into the conversation and gathered that John was trying to move them on to another group of guests.

'I know Richard is a new face and a very handsome one too, but you mustn't monopolise him, Sasha—'

Sasha opened her mouth to protest. No way was she monopolising the stranger! And he—*Richard*—was smiling indulgently again. She frothed inside. Henrietta's daggers were still drawn.

'I'll join you in a minute,' he told John and Henrietta firmly. 'I haven't finished with Sasha yet—no, not by a long way.'

If looks could have killed, Richard and Sasha alongside him would have been prostrate on the floor. Henrietta was furious; her uncle simply nodded and guided his niece away from them, and Sasha wondered what power this man beside her had over John Harvey. It was obvious that he wanted to circulate his niece and the stranger but the stranger was having none of it.

Sasha turned to him when John and his abominable niece were out of earshot, her eyes narrowed with pent-up frustration.

'Don't say it,' he said under his breath. 'You're quite capable of fighting your own battles—'

'You took the words out of my mouth. I sincerely hope that you are not expecting my undying gratitude because—'

'I didn't think there would be any hope of it,' he said on a theatrical sigh. 'Now, perhaps, we can forget that you have probably made a lifelong enemy of the niece of the most powerful man on the island—'

'Just a minute!' Sasha breathed angrily. 'If I've made any enemies it wasn't without help from you. Where the hell did this begging business come from? You! Now, I don't know what sort of games you are playing with the Hun's affections but she sees me as a threat and I didn't ask for that—no, not one bit—'

'Henrietta and I are friends—'

'And Christmas falls in July!' Sasha spat contemptuously. She held up her palms to the stranger as if to ward him off; at the same time she shook her head. 'Look, I'm not interested in your love life. I'm not interested in you or the Hun; just leave me alone.' With that she spun away from him and he didn't stop her this time.

With eyes still burning with rage and the indignities she'd suffered she swept across the room to find Todd and tell him that she was leaving. She'd walk back to the hospital complex on her own. She'd had enough.

'Richard is one of the Carltons of Auckland...' Sasha heard the voice of Henrietta expounding proudly to someone. She stopped dead in her tracks on the wide veranda that surrounded the villa. She had searched everywhere for Todd and this was her last hope. The mention of the name Carlton had her flattening her back against a crimson bougainvillea sprawling up one of the posts of the veranda.

'Richard's seriously wealthy in his own right, of course—made zillions in South America and is looking to invest his money here on the islands,' Henrietta was saying. 'But, to be honest, what he's seen so far hasn't inspired him with much confidence.'

Sasha heard the blur of Todd's voice in response but none of the words registered, not one. Several words from Henrietta had registered, though; like knives they scoured under her flesh, leaving her gasping with shock. Richard Carlton, 'one of the Carltons of Auckland'...'South America'... Dear God, this couldn't be possible. She'd wake up and find it had been a nightmare...

She leaned back and a splinter of wood from the post stabbed her arm. In horror she stared at the pinprick of blood oozing from her burning skin.

She was awake and it wasn't a nightmare; it was worse—a living nightmare. The stranger she had crossed swords with was *Geoff's brother*! The one she had never met. The one who had been in South America making his 'zillions' while the wedding plans were going through. The one who had been returning to New Zealand to be best man at his younger brother's wedding at the very time that Sasha had made her terrible discovery.

As she sped through the hot, humid night her heart pounded and she cried inwardly over and over again, The world isn't big enough, dammit; it just isn't!

CHAPTER TWO

THE morning sun scorched the top of Sasha's head the next day as she beached the canoe and dragged it up the sands away from the shoreline. Thank heavens she'd seen sense earlier and not insisted on bringing the generator back with her. It was weightier than expected and two of the boys from the maintenance staff at the hospital had promised to bring it over later and help her set it up.

The chatter of parakeets and cockatoos welcomed her ashore and Sasha let out a small sigh of relief as she walked slowly up the beach to the bungalow, dragging the oilskin capes behind her. The island always had this effect on her—it had a soporific tranquillity that wrapped around her comfortingly.

The palms on the beach swayed a gentle welcome to her and Sasha smiled. She felt safe here, protected by isolation, cloaked by the steamy heat of the tiny island that only she and Ruth and a multitude of wildlife inhabited.

Richard Carlton. His name wouldn't leave her mind and she resented it very strongly—any intrusion into her inner peace she resented. And she had found peace here on this crazy little island that was paradise on days like this and Hades on earth when the rains and the cyclones came.

Richard Carlton—here to look for investment possibilities, not her, she repeated resolutely to herself. He

didn't know who she was and never would. She'd
changed her name. She was Sasha Thompson now, not
Letitia McKenzie. And there was no reason for him to
be looking for her anyway, she persuaded herself as she
flopped down on the top step of the veranda and leaned
her burning head against a post.

Her past—she didn't want to be reminded of it but it
rose like a phoenix out of the recesses of her mind, and
all because of Geoff's brother appearing out of nowhere, transported to her refuge by a Chinese trader and
here for a month or more.

She might be able to avoid him but knew deep down
that it was inevitable that they would meet again. The
islands were so small that everyone knew each other.
Their paths would cross again and the thought filled her
with despair.

Was he as pushy as his brother? Geoff had pursued
her relentlessly, overwhelmed her with his attentions till
she had believed herself in love and agreed to marry him.
The two families had been delighted and it had only been
on that last, fateful day before the wedding that she had
found out the truth.

It shuddered through her now—the unwelcome intrusion of her past—biting through the heat and tranquillity of her tiny island and hurling her back in time.

She had been happy, armed with parcels and the small
glass figurine she had bought for Geoff as a pre-wedding
gift. Not expensive—they both came from wealthy families and could afford the best—the glass ornament, a
crystal clown with an expression of fun on his grinning
face, had captured her heart. Geoff was fun; he grabbed
at life with both hands and lived it to the full. The clown
was fun; the clown was Geoff. He'd love it.

She'd let herself into his penthouse apartment, not really expecting him to be there as there was so much to do before the wedding the next day—the mega-expensive wedding that would bind two of the most influential families of Auckland together for life. Their children would be Carlton McKenzies; their dynasties would be irrevocably bonded.

Sasha, smiling happily, had unwrapped the clown and placed it tenderly on the antique chiffonier by the answering machine, knowing it would be the first place he would go when he got home from the Carlton offices. Then she had heard a sound—a small sound which she could not identify. It had lifted her heart for a second, though, because it meant that Geoff was home and she could give him the clown personally and see for herself his delight.

She opened the bedroom door and in that fleeting glance into the room her heart stopped. The world stopped. Frozen in terror and shock, she took in the whole appalling scene but nothing registered—nothing but a pain so deep and wounding that a cry shot out from her lips. It was an animal sound of despair that was only heard by herself.

Geoff was naked, straddling the body of a woman— a woman with long blonde hair who writhed and giggled beneath him. Geoff was laughing too—a strange laugh that she had never heard before. They were completely unaware that she was standing in the doorway, frozen to the spot as if a life force outside their own had para-lysed her.

Only Sasha's wide green eyes functioned, moving frantically from the couple to the bedside table, to the floor, to the paraphernalia that littered both—silver paper, straws, a powdery residue left on the gleaming glass surface of the table...

Blindly she reached the front door, only aware of a terrible pounding in her head and a deep sickness inside her that burned and burned.

Geoff caught her as her fingers scrabbled helplessly at the lock. He flung her back against the door and trapped her there with his hands pressed against the panelling at each side of her head. His eyes were dilated, his breath hot; beads of nervous perspiration broke out on his brow. She heard his voice screaming at her—jumbled words that only afterwards became clear.

'You don't understand...it isn't what it seems... Everyone does it these days!'

Then came the harsh, icy wind of reality and Sasha's head was suddenly clear, her mind calm and lucid. She stared at Geoff, her eyes as hard and glittering as emeralds, and he knew—knew the great mistake he had made. His fear was palpable.

'Don't you dare—just don't you dare breathe a word of this to anyone, Letitia,' he growled furiously. 'This would kill my father; it would destroy him!'

No words of sorrow for her; no regrets that she should have witnessed such a thing; nothing but concern for what his father might think.

'Forget you ever came here,' he blurted out in panic. His hands came down and raked through his hair and he turned away from her as if he couldn't face her any more.

Sasha stared at him then, seeing him as he really was for the very first time—a weak, pathetic creature dominated by the power of his father. A towel hung around his waist—such a feeble attempt at propriety for her benefit, a cover-up, as if it mattered after what she had seen. She knew now that that was how her life would be with him—one big cover-up.

He turned back to her as she stood in silence watching him, her face shocked into an expression of impassiveness. His eyes suddenly blazed like twin fires.

'And don't look at me like that!' he roared, and Sasha flinched. 'You don't know the pressure I'm under... This...this marriage is essential! My father *needs* this marriage, this...this coupling of the two families.'

His strength zapped out of him so suddenly that Sasha flinched once again. His whole body sagged and when he lifted his head his eyes were glassy.

'It's going to be all right,' he croaked, licking his dry lips. 'We are going to be all right, Letitia. You saw nothing; you know nothing.' His eyes pleaded with hers. 'I promise you, darling, it's going to be all right.' He took her shoulders and she tensed under his grasp, knowing it would never be all right, not ever. And he knew too.

His grip tightened painfully. 'We are going to be married tomorrow, Letitia; it's all arranged and nothing, but nothing, is going to stop us. Forget the drugs, that tart; it didn't happen... Believe me, it didn't happen.'

With very little effort she shrugged his hands from her shoulders. She turned and coolly opened the door and her silent attempt to leave him had him exploding with rage. He stood in the doorway, screaming at her as she walked resolutely down the corridor to the lift.

'You betray me and you and your father and that social-climbing stepmother of yours will suffer, I promise you. I'll destroy all of you if one word of this gets out!'

* * *

Sasha let out a wounded cry of hopelessness that scattered the birds from the pawpaw tree. She bit her lip and squeezed her eyes tight shut against the bitter memories that were swamping her. Slowly she stood up and stared out to sea. A warm breeze lifted the hair from her throbbing head and it soothed her slightly.

It seemed that her past had caught up with her in the form of Geoff's brother but she knew that mustn't make a crisis out of his appearance on the islands. She had covered her tracks well. No one here knew who she really was.

She had written to her father, telling him of her change of name and how she wanted to build a new life for herself. She had told him nothing of what she had seen that day in Geoff's apartment; fear had held the truth back. She had simply said that she had changed her mind and didn't want to marry Geoff after all.

The last sighting of Letitia McKenzie had been in Singapore two years previously, then the media had lost interest. It had been through the media that she had found out exactly what Geoff had said about her after she had left. Her father had sent her the cuttings and she had burned them. The stories were so sickeningly painful that she knew she could never return.

Sasha went inside the bungalow, made tea and brought it out onto the shady veranda to drink. She was on her second cup when she heard the distant drone of an engine approaching across the reef. She was feeling better, much more settled now that she had convinced herself that nothing could touch her again. If she ever ran into Richard Carlton again she could handle him.

She ran down the beach to greet the approaching canoe, excited that the boys had come so promptly with the generator. The sun was full in her face so she couldn't see that there was only one occupant till it was closer.

'I don't believe this,' Sasha hissed under her breath, her blood running cold at the sight of Richard Carlton expertly negotiating the coral reef so close to the shore. What the hell was he doing here?

'A bit tricky, that,' he admitted as he cut the engine and sprang over the side of the canoe to haul it out of the water. 'They warned me the reef was a nasty one. Any chance of a medal for bravery?'

His supercilious grin was as wide as the ocean and inwardly Sasha raged at it. Oh, yes, he was Geoff's brother all right. Overnight she had challenged it in her mind, praying that she might have made a mistake and misheard the hideous Henrietta. But the evidence had been overwhelming.

But she was overreacting now and she calmed herself. He was nothing like Geoff, in looks or character. Even in arrogance this man was streets ahead of his younger brother.

'No chance,' Sasha muttered as she closed in on the canoe to peer inside it. There lay her generator. 'What goes on?' she asked, lifting her head to look at him. His hair was wild and wind-blown, his T-shirt wet with sea spray, his shorts oily, as if he'd done battle with the out-board engine at some stage. She recognised the canoe as one of the hospital's.

'I couldn't bear the thought of a day without your waspish charm to needle some life into my bones. You make an exhilarating change from Henrietta's waspish tongue, which I'm quite immune to now.'

'Glutton for punishment, aren't you?'

'True, I have a masochistic streak to me—a curious one too. I want to see how a girl Friday lives. I could use a beer too.'

Sasha ignored him and leaned into the canoe to see if she could shift the generator.

His hand locked over hers, stilling it. The sensation was electrifying. She pulled free and glared at him.

'That can wait; my thirst can't. After you.' He gestured for her to go ahead of him.

She did, simply because it was less effort than to argue that she didn't want him on her island and he should buzz off back to Kula.

'No beer,' she threw over her shoulder. 'I don't drink it so have no need to keep it in.'

'What about Ruth? Is she teetotal too?'

Sasha frowned but strode on. He knew that she shared the bungalow with Ruth and he could only know that if he'd asked. It seemed that he knew far too much about her already to be healthy.

'Afraid so,' she sang. 'So what are you doing here?' she asked when they reached the steps of the veranda. She was making an enormous effort to sound normal. She hoped it was working because her heart was still thudding dangerously at his unexpected appearance.

'I told you, I wanted to see how you lived. Isn't that enough for you?'

'No, it isn't. Why?' She held his look with coldly suspicious eyes.

He shrugged. 'Because.'

'Because what?' she persisted. He didn't answer, just smiled enigmatically as if he knew something she didn't. It was a smile that chilled Sasha to the bone. Surely he couldn't know the truth about her? No one here did.

She turned from him, ran up the steps and through the bead curtains that kept the flies out of the bungalow. Act normal, she repeated stoically to herself; don't act as if you have something to hide and he might go away.

'OK, this is it,' she told him, swinging to face him. 'Humble but home. This is how Girl Friday lives. Look, real furniture, not a pile of earth to sit on. That is actually a television in the corner, not a cardboard box painted to look like one. We use it for videos. Oh, and this is a telephone; you know, the sort that rings.

'And in the bathroom there is a shower with real water and I have magical powers to make it hot too; I just flick a switch and hey presto. I have a fridge as well with a *real* icebox. Isn't it amazing how civilised one can live in this land of "barbarians"?'

He said nothing. He was good at that—saying nothing. The trouble was that that cynical smile of his said a lot. She could be as caustic and sarcastic as she liked and it didn't bother him.

'Icebox, hmm?' he muttered at last. 'That sounds like there might be some drinkable water around.'

Sasha took the hint and went through to the narrow kitchen. He followed and watched her, unnerving her as she poured water and added ice. She handed it to him and he took it, their eyes making contact over the rim of the glass.

She felt that chill again and didn't want him there. He disturbed her and she knew why. It had nothing, but nothing, to do with him being an attractive man. He was Geoff's brother and her past was her past, gone for ever, and she wanted no reminders.

'Be careful going back through that coral reef,' she advised. If that wasn't a big enough hint to push off again, she didn't know what was. 'You were lucky to get here without scraping the hull; you might not be so lucky going back. The light is different going out to sea,' she added.

'I'm staying,' he told her coolly after downing the water.

Sasha stared at him, stupefied by that remark. If he knew that she shared this home with Ruth then he more than likely knew that Ruth was away. He might even have seen her leaving yesterday morning from Kula. He *knew* she was alone here. What else did he know?

She recovered quickly, 'If you want to stay I go,' she told him decisively.

'Why so frosty?' he asked.

'Why so pushy?' she shot back.

He folded his arms across his chest. 'Am I being pushy?'

Sasha braced herself. She was getting nowhere. 'Very pushy. Last night you were over the top, using me in your little love games with Henrietta. This morning you are here, in my space.' Her green eyes bored into his. 'I've got one nerve left and you are leaning on it.'

He smiled, not at all worried by her veiled warnings. 'They said you were a tough cookie with no soft centre. I'm beginning to believe them.'

Sasha felt pain stab deep inside her at the knowledge of what people thought of her. But it wasn't an insult, she persuaded herself; a bit of a compliment, actually.

'I have to be tough in my job,' she told him, not in the least bit curious to know where he'd got his information from. Gossip was rife on the islands.

'Do you have to be quite so tough in your private life as well?' His voice had softened slightly and Sasha was on red alert.

'Why don't you mind your own business?' she told him, and snatched the glass from his hand and rinsed it under the tap.

'You are my business at the moment,' he said quietly. 'We're going to be spending a lot of time together and backbiting can get tiresome after a while. You coming down off your high horse will go a long way to making it all more pleasurable.'

His words hung like leaden cobwebs in the slightly musty atmosphere of the kitchen. Sasha stopped what she was doing and slowly turned to him. This man wasn't getting the message, not one bit. She didn't want him here but he was so determined that it was almost frightening.

'Look, Mr Carlton, I'm not even flattered that you want to spend time with me. I'm not interested in you. I have no desire to spend any longer than is necessary in your company and if you think you can come here and persuade me otherwise you are very much mistaken. I'm not attracted to you—'

'How did you know my surname was Carlton?' he interrupted coolly.

Sasha was stunned into silence by the question because it was so unexpected—unexpected and unnerving because it suggested that his name might mean something to her. It did, of course, but did he know that?

'Have you been making enquiries about me?' he persisted.

Sasha found her voice. 'No way!' she said heatedly. 'You forget, we were introduced to each other last night.'

'We were not,' he said quietly. 'When John came over he presumed that we had already made our own introductions. My Christian name was mentioned but certainly not my surname.'

Sasha huffed and turned away again, hoping that she wasn't colouring with embarrassment. Then she remembered that he had known her name too. So had he overheard something said about her as well? Probably. Gossip again.

'So how did you know?' he asked.

'Does it matter?' she said on a sigh of boredom.

'It does. I'd like to think you were interested enough to find out more about me.'

'Wrong. Sorry to disappoint you but I overheard someone talking about you. Satisfied?'

He was eyeing her curiously, eyes narrowed, as she turned back to him.

He said, 'It will do,' though he didn't sound convinced.

'It will have to!'

He nodded. 'So let's get back to where you were. You're not attracted to me; anything else you'd like to add to that?'

Sasha eyed him warily, wishing that she hadn't said anything about being attracted; the denial implied that she just might be. 'This is all getting out of hand,' she told him frostily. 'You are wasting my time and your own. Thank you for bringing my generator over; now you can go.'

He glanced at his watch and straightened up from the work surface he had been leaning on. 'Yes, I ought to get back and pack my stuff. I'll be back later.'

'Excuse me,' she blurted out hurriedly, her eyes wide, 'but what an earth for?'

'To help you fix the generator for one thing,' he said as if she should know that. 'Talking of which, it is rather heavy. Could you give me a hand with it?'

The generator! She'd completely forgotten about it. And why had *he* brought it and not the boys? She asked as she followed him out onto the veranda.

'I told you, I was curious to see how you lived and so offered my services. Now I'm satisfied and—'

'You don't need to bother coming back again,' Sasha interjected quickly.

He laughed as he strode down the beach to the canoe, Sasha having to trot to keep up with him.

'Sorry to disappoint *you*, but I'll be back.' He stopped by the canoe and turned to her. 'This trip was to look over the lie of the land. I like what I see. I'll be back.' His eyes flicked over her, up then down, taking in her shabby shorts, worn vest-top, and the exceedingly tatty espadrilles which hung on her feet by a whisper and a prayer.

Sasha knew that she looked her worst but this wasn't Waikiki Beach. However, by the look of pure sexual appraisal he was giving her it was as if she were one of those golden beauties who strutted their stuff on the shoreline. For that look she would have ordered him off the island instantly but she needed that generator.

She took one end of it and together they lifted it out of the canoe.

'If you do come...back,' she huffed as they carried the generator up the beach, 'you'll...you'll get the same tone of welcome as the first time.'

'You mean you're capable of fixing this up yourself?'

'Yes, quite capable but...but thank you for the offer anyway.' It was remarkable how he wasn't even breaking

out in a sweat carrying this load. She'd have one hell of
a job getting it into position, but she'd manage, and no
way was she going to let him know that it might be a
struggle.

'Where do you want it?'

'Round...the back. There's a lean-to.'

They heaved it round the back and gently placed it
down under the shade of the wooden lean-to. The
shrunken, sun-bleached fronds of the palm roof let in
a dappled shade that cast shadows across their faces. He
looked darker and more threatening in the dim light and
Sasha wondered at herself for noticing.

'Thanks,' she breathed heavily.

'Don't touch it till I get back. It's far too heavy for
you to manhandle on your own.'

'Look, Mr Carlton—'

'Richard. Not Dick or Richie or Ricky. Good old-
fashioned Richard will do just fine.'

'Well, good old-fashioned Richard,' she drawled sarcastically, 'I'm just a good old-fashioned girl, so forget
coming back later. I don't need your help and I don't
need you in my bed. Got the message?'

'Ah, but I don't think *you've* quite got the message.'

Sasha was suddenly aware of a distinct change in his
tone. Gone was the mockery; it was dead serious.

'I'm not looking to leap into your bed and I'm getting
a little bored by your abrasive manner and your blind
assumption that I'm after your body. I shall be returning later, with or without your permission, with or
without your approval. You'd better get used to the idea
because it is going to happen. Have I made myself clear?'

'Quite,' she told him coldly, though she was boiling
inside at his arrogance. 'Your intentions are immovable

so you had better take mine into consideration. You can come back any time you damned like. You can paddle over here, sit on the beach, swim amongst the dolphins, think beautiful thoughts, but what you can't do is come into my house—'

'Whose house?' His dark brow rose questioningly.

Apprehension suddenly skidded down her spine. It wasn't her house and he knew. Another sensation trickled down her back. He was being unbelievably persistent and she wondered why. For a second a real fear hit her—that maybe he did know who she was. She fought it, trying to evaporate it from her mind, but it clung on like mist in a rainforest.

He couldn't know, she persisted, and besides, there was absolutely no reason for him to be here even if he did know... which he didn't... he didn't.

She ran her tongue over her very dry lips before speaking in a croaky whisper. 'I...I might not own it but I live here and have a right to my privacy.' Her confidence was sliding perilously because of the way he was looking at her, so sublimely confident that whatever she said meant absolutely nothing.

'John Harvey owns this property,' he told her smoothly. 'I'm John Harvey's guest.'

'And...and what is that supposed to mean?' Her voice was barely a whisper again.

His wasn't. It came out loud and clear and very deliberate.

'It means that I'm coming to stay. For the next few weeks I shall be *your* house guest, not John's.'

After delivering that little gem he turned and ducked out of the lean-to and left her standing in the dappled shade, almost too weak to move. Sweeping her hair wildly from her face, she suddenly strode after him and caught him at the front of the veranda.

'Perhaps you'd better tell me what exactly is going on.'

'I thought you'd never ask,' he drawled sarcastically.

'Look, this isn't the time for playing games—'

'I never was playing games, Sasha. You've been the one getting a buzz out of our altercations.'

She stared at him in disbelief at his insight. It was far more acute than hers. She *had* been getting a buzz out of their cut and thrust. Astonishingly it was true. What she didn't understand was why, though. That would take time to analyse—time she didn't have at the moment.

'So now it's serious,' she murmured. 'Tell me exactly what is going on.'

'Exactly what is going on is that I'm coming to stay, here on this island.' He waved a vague hand at the bungalow. 'I've inspected the accommodation and it's a pleasant surprise. Quite civilised enough for my needs and—'

'But this is ridiculous!' Sasha protested. 'Struth, she was hot, burning up inside and out. 'You can't possibly come and stay here. This is my home—'

'But not your property. The house belongs to John and he allows you to use it because he rather likes you and appreciates the work you do for the hospital. Now I need somewhere to stay while I'm here—'

'You have somewhere to stay!' she screeched. 'You and Henrietta are staying with him in his...in his *palace*—which it is compared to this,' she reasoned hotly. 'You must be mad! If I had the choice I know where I'd rather be; I'd—'

'But it isn't your choice, you see, it's mine. I want to be here and John thinks it's a good idea and Henrietta—'

'Oh, no! Absolutely not! There is no way I'll share my home with the Hun!' She actually stamped her espadrilled foot in the crunchy sand. 'You bring her here and I'm off!'

His eyes glinted with a sudden humour. 'So you approve of *me* coming?'

'No...no, I didn't mean that.' She was flustered, feeling shivers of despair now. She felt she was losing some sort of battle here. True, the place belonged to John and he could put anyone he liked in it, but surely not this terrible twosome?

'Henrietta won't be accompanying me; in fact she thinks the whole idea stinks. That's probably what's making me more determined to do it.'

Sasha shook her head in disbelief. 'My God, you sophisticates are something. Why don't you go back where you belong and play your puerile games amongst your own? They are very misplaced here.

'So, let's get the facts on file. You intend staying here in my house—sorry, John's house, and with his approval—mine obviously doesn't matter. The fact that I've lived here for nearly two years doesn't even give me squatters' rights, apparently. OK, fact. You want to stay here; you are determined to stay here.

'Now this must come across as a bit of a *barbarian* question to ask someone like yourself but, for God's sake, why?'

'Now that is something we can discuss over dinner later because I really ought to be getting back.' He glanced at his watch again and turned away down the beach towards his canoe. Sasha was not going to be fobbed off with that—a nothing answer to a very straightforward question.

'You are being totally unreasonable,' she fumed as he started to push the canoe into the water. 'You come here expecting me to welcome you with open arms into my home. No reason, just a whim on your part—'

'Oh, there is every reason. I don't do anything without a reason.' He smiled knowingly at her as he leapt into the bobbing canoe, picking up the paddle to propel himself into deeper water before starting the outboard. 'There is method in my madness.'

Oh, dear God, he did know who she was! He was here to torment her, to torture her for what she had done to his brother.

'So you admit you are mad?' she shouted out defensively as he drew away from her. She was almost dancing up and down with frustration and her heart thudded out her fear of his reasons for wanting to come back. She wanted answers and now. Why was he pursuing her so?

'Very likely,' he called back. 'Anything I can bring over for you?'

'Forget it . . .'

She suddenly had an idea. He wasn't—no, he wasn't going to have the last word on this. Taking a big breath to carry her words over the slap of his paddle in the water, she shouted, 'Forget it because I won't be here! You can have the house and I hope the midges eat you alive. I don't care because I won't be here!'

His paddle stilled. 'What was that?' he called.

She had him! Joyfully she cupped her hands round her mouth. 'I said I won't be here. I've a room in the hospital complex. You here, me there. Perfect!'

He laughed. He actually laughed and shook his head.

'Sorry to disappoint you, sweetheart, but you haven't a room in any hospital complex; in fact you haven't a job—'

'What?' she screamed hysterically, positively frothing with rage now. 'What do you mean I haven't a job?' It suddenly hit her that Henrietta had disliked her on sight, but surely he hadn't used her influence with the hospital board, on which her uncle sat, to get her sacked? And then a worse thought shuddered through her. Richard Carlton *did* know who she was and *he'd* scuppered her job with the hospital!

'Don't worry about it. I'll explain everything when I get back. Over and out.' He started the outboard and all further communication was shut out by the roar of the engine.

Sasha was left jumping up and down on the broken coral, shaking her fists and screaming her rage like one of the barbarians of a long-ago age. She'd shrink his head for this; yes, she would, if only she knew how!

CHAPTER THREE

SASHA was still fuming hours later. She'd swum herself senseless, beachcombed till she was rigid with boredom, trekked through the rainforest that rose up behind the bungalow till the midges had driven her home again, but she was still fuming.

What was his game? Just what was he up to? He couldn't stay here; it was impossible, and why? He *did* know who she was and had come to punish her for what she had done to his wretched brother, for having jilted him on the day before their wedding.

But Geoff had already had his revenge and could do no more damage and two years was a long time. He'd probably courted another eligible heiress by now and was married, so there was no reason, none at all, for his brother to seek her out. But he was being alarmingly persistent and that worried her greatly.

She toyed with the phone later that afternoon. She could call John Harvey and put herself out of this misery but the phone was supplied by the hospital for emergencies only, and though this was an emergency to her the hospital board wouldn't see it that way.

She was waiting on the beach much later in the day as he approached with another loaded canoe in tow. She helped him pull them ashore. Her anger hadn't abated with the heat of the long day but her fear she had under control. The man couldn't be hell-bent on revenge; there was no reason to hurt her any more. She'd been punished enough for something she hadn't done. But, of course, this Carlton didn't know the truth and family ties were—Stop it!

Her anger erupted in reaction to her fears and she started on him as soon as they had the canoes clear of the foaming surf.

'How dare you just go off like that this morning, leaving me to worry myself sick all day? What did you mean I have no job?'

'Can't it wait till later? I'd like to get settled in before nightfall.'

'No, it can't wait,' Sasha responded and her voice cracked as she spoke. She'd had a terrible day of frustration and worry and the oppressive heat of late afternoon was taking its toll of her energy resources. She realised that she hadn't eaten and now she was hungry and he was just too much.

She was surprised to see a look of concern for her darken his eyes. Concern she didn't need. She snatched at a holdall he'd humped out of the second canoe and started back up the beach with it.

'Leave that,' he called out frostily. 'I might need your services in some areas but I don't expect you to porter for me.'

She dropped the bag and turned to him, for his benefit her face a mask of indifference. 'Suit yourself. I was only trying to be helpful, as I can see I'm not going to get anything out of you till you've got your feet well and truly under my table.'

'Ah, you've softened,' he said, with a sarcastic smile.

No smiles from Sasha. 'Nothing of the sort. I just want some answers, sooner rather than later, but as it's obvious you lack any sort of consideration for anyone but yourself I'll just have to bite bullets.'

She heard his soft laughter as she dragged her weary self back to the bungalow, where she somewhat lethargically busied herself in the kitchen making herself something to eat.

It took him several trips to bring his stuff up from the canoes and neither spoke till he stood in the middle of the sitting room, surrounded by bags and packages. There were camera cases and photographic equipment, a video camera, several hold-alls, a dusty briefcase that was very out of place, and, of all things, a video recorder.

There were boxes of groceries too; obviously a fussy eater, Sasha thought as she surveyed the pile of his belongings at his feet.

She was standing in the open doorway of the kitchen and he was standing in the middle of the sitting room and she suddenly thought how ludicrous all this was. Yesterday her life had been simple and uncomplicated; today, thanks to him, her nerves were wavering on the edge of insanity.

'What on earth is all that?' she asked.

'Everything I need for my stay,' he told her, lifting his personal holdall. 'Do I have a choice of bedrooms?'

She stared at him, too stricken for words. It was really happening; he was expecting to share her home with her. After what he had said earlier she didn't even have the option of escaping to the hospital complex to fall back on. She shook her head and calmed herself and spoke at last.

'Please tell me what is going on. You aren't being fair.'

He let the holdall drop to the polished floor and slowly came towards her. Sasha tensed as he stopped in front of her. She thought he was going to touch her, reach out and place his hands on her shoulders, but he didn't.

'I'm sorry if you think I'm not being fair, but you do rather ask for it. If for just one minute you'd drop your defences we might get somewhere,' he told her calmly. 'You are cold and abrasive, prickly and abusive; you have a negative attitude to me and you have hardly given me a chance to explain everything in full. If I wind you up it is your own doing. You wind *me* up. Does any of that register with you?'

Sasha widened her eyes. All true. She was everything he said. She shrugged.

'Yes, it registers, but if you are expecting an apology you can forget it,' she told him equally calmly. 'I work here on the islands and I live here and enjoy my life. You have suddenly disrupted it. I don't like being flirted with, I don't like being accused of begging by your girl-friend, I don't like having my privacy invaded and I don't like having my job threatened by a stranger who has only been on the islands for a day. Does any of that register with *you*?'

He lowered his head hopelessly for a second and then he looked up at her. 'Perhaps we had better start all over again,' he suggested with a sudden warmth to his tone.

Sasha eyed him warily. She was trying so hard to think reasonably but it wasn't easy when she knew who he was, though who he was shouldn't have made any dif-ference. He wasn't his brother but could be of the same mould; she didn't know that but wasn't giving him a chance anyway.

She reminded herself that he had angered her *before* she had found out his identity. And that wasn't her fault.

Geoff had done that to her, made her wary of any man, and that was her problem, not Richard Carlton's.

She let out a small, silent sigh and met his eyes full-on. 'OK, I agree; let's start over. I'll ask you a few simple questions and you give me a few simple answers.'

He nodded. 'Fire away.'

'My job—that's most important so we'll start with that. What did you mean I haven't got one?'

'For the moment you haven't,' he told her bluntly. 'You're on leave for a month, or maybe longer if I need to be here longer. You are due the leave and as you seemed reluctant to take it I moved things along for you.'

'So, you've arranged my leave and want me off this island so you can take up residence.' Sasha shrugged hopelessly. It seemed that he had some sort of influence over the hospital board and, apparently, John Harvey.

'Yes, I've arranged your leave for you but I certainly don't want you off the island. I need you here.'

'I'm a hospital administrator, not a housekeeper.'

He shook his head. 'I'm not expecting you to keep house for me. I think we can share the household chores. I'm not averse to a bit of cleaning and cooking. I need your assistance for a while and John agrees you deserve a break and we worked things out very satisfactorily.'

'Without even consulting me,' she argued, not fiercely, though. She seemed to have little fight left in her. Harvey's influence on the islands was immense. He always got what he wanted because he talked money, but this was the first time she had been personally affected by it.

'You didn't need to be consulted. I make the decisions,' he told her.

Sasha turned away from him and stepped back into the kitchen. He came and stood behind her as she picked up a tomato and sliced through it thoughtfully. She was determined to stay calm over this, to a certain degree. Losing her temper didn't help; she'd quickly learnt that to her cost and frustration.

'Do you have any more questions?' he asked from behind her.

She carried on slicing, giving a small shrug. 'Yes, many. I'm just a bit stunned for the minute. I don't take too kindly to being manipulated. I do my job well and I take my leave when it suits the hospital, not John Harvey.'

She felt him touch her shoulder to turn her to face him and she tensed so hard that his hand immediately dropped. She faced him of her own free will and was surprised to see a look of concern creasing his brow.

'You really are upset at the idea of sharing your home with me.'

'Yes, I am,' she admitted honestly. 'But more than that I would have liked to have been asked, and what is worse is that I can't just walk out and tell you and John to go take a jump at yourselves. I love my work and the hospital needs John's funding, and I have to kowtow to the pair of you if I want to stay employed and want the hospital to flourish. I see that as some sort of blackmail and I don't like it.'

'It makes you feel vulnerable, does it?'

'Vulnerable *and* unappreciated.'

'You are certainly not unappreciated. John is very aware of how hard you work and what you have done for the hospital—'

'Well, he has a funny way of showing it.'

'Your job will be there for you when I've finished with you.' He smiled as he spoke as if a smile would make it all right. Well, one of his cutting smiles she could live without.

Sasha gave him a smirk of derision. The patience she was forcing on herself was wearing threadbare.

'I'll tell you something: at this precise moment I feel like resigning and moving off—'

'To where?' he interrupted. 'Running does no good.'

Sasha felt a small thread of apprehension tighten inside her. He'd said that as if he'd known that she'd fled from something in the past. She gave herself a mental shake. Of course he didn't know. She was scaring herself with suppositions like that. He did *not* know.

'So what exactly do you need me for if it isn't to pander to your needs while you are here?'

'You will show me around.'

She smirked again and turned back to the salad she was preparing. 'There isn't a lot to see. This house is the only one. There's a beach that surrounds the island and—'

'Not just here. I want to see all this group of islands. From now on you're my guide.'

She turned back to him, wondering how he had persuaded John to give over her precious time to the whims of a wealthy tourist wanting to see the sights.

'Why me?' she gasped in exasperation.

'Because you know the islands—'

'So do all the islanders,' Sasha protested, waving the knife she was holding. 'There are hundreds of them out there who'd be only too willing to earn a few dollars to be your guide.' She slammed the knife down in a temper. 'This is ridiculous—'

'It isn't ridiculous at all,' he interrupted insistently. 'I don't speak pidgin, you do, and besides, I'd value your opinion *en route*.'

With a cynical laugh Sasha blurted out, 'My opinion on what—suitable souvenirs to take back for your friends?' She shook her head in disbelief. He'd said that this wasn't ridiculous but it damned well was.

'This isn't a pleasure trip, Sasha.'

'Oh, no? What is it, then?'

'A business trip.'

'A business trip?' she echoed, eyes narrowing. 'What sort of business trip?'

'Wouldn't you rather discuss it over dinner?' he suggested wearily. 'I'm quite hungry and I'd like to unpack and take a shower if that's all right with you. Now, where is my bedroom?'

Sasha couldn't answer straight away. Her throat felt thick and blocked with frustration. He was here to stay and there was apparently nothing she could do about it, and the thought needled and needled till she thought she must be bleeding internally. Why him, why her, why in this small corner of the world where she had sought escape had this man come to haunt her?

He didn't wait for her answer. She watched through the doorway as he started to gather up armfuls of his belongings. If he hadn't been a Carlton she might have felt some sort of exhilaration at the prospect of acting as his guide for a few weeks, not because he was an attractive man but because...

Her heart recoiled at her thoughts. He *was* an attractive man. He was also arrogant and forceful, got what he wanted any which way he could, but, overwhelmingly, he was an attractive-*looking* man. Ruth would undoubtedly adore him. Sasha never could and never would—of that she was determined.

'That's my bedroom,' she called out to him as he was about to open her door. He stopped and she crossed the sitting room, gathering up one of his bags as she went. 'This one—Ruth's room,' she told him, opening the door next to hers for him. He walked through and grimaced at the sight of the bed opposite the window with its protective covering of mosquito netting.

'I'll never get used to sleeping under one of those,' he commented as he dumped his bags in the corner by the bathroom door.

'Surely you had them in South America?'

She could have bitten her tongue out at that slip-up. He was onto it as quickly as she had expected.

'So you *have* been checking up on me. I'm flattered.'

She could have slapped the smirk from his face. 'Don't be,' she told him flippantly. 'It was another snippet of conversation I overheard.'

'Did you overhear anything else that might affect us?'

She gave him a dazzling smile. 'Nothing about you affects me, Richard.'

'I've made you mad at times, though. I affect you that way. I wonder why?'

She didn't like the inflexion in the question but chose to ignore it. She didn't want to be on a personal level with him. She changed the subject.

'Just one thing before I leave you to settle... There is quite a hefty staff at the hospital and any number of them could have been your guide. Why me?'

'Are you fishing for a compliment?' He was wandering around the room, inspecting the simple cane furniture.

'I wasn't, actually. I was just curious to know why John offered me up as the sacrificial lamb.'

He stopped his wanderings and looked at her with hooded dark eyes. 'Do you really want to know?'

That look worried her and suddenly she didn't want to know, whatever the reason.

'I'll tell you,' he added, 'and then, perhaps, it will be the end of any speculation on your part.'

The words were so damned meaningful that Sasha drew in her breath. The creep actually thought that she might be flattered or, worse, actually interested in the possibility that he had personally asked for her.

'You're expendable,' was all he added, but the brutality with which he loaded the words hit Sasha below the belt.

She went cold inside and it must have showed in her face because he came across the room to her and took hold of her shoulders. She tensed at the contact but this time he didn't let her go.

'You're a strange one—so hard and brittle and yet you have the capability to be hurt so easily.' His voice was low and verging on soothing but it did little to put Sasha's mind at rest. She preferred him arrogant and mocking. It was safer that way.

She stepped back out of his light grasp and his hands dropped to his side, and he shrugged slightly as if her reluctance for any contact between them didn't much matter to him. It was strange but in that second she had the strong feeling that he wasn't personally interested in her at all, that all his flirting—when she came to think of it now there hadn't been much of it anyway—had meant absolutely nothing. It was a relief in a way but there again...

'I don't mean to dent your ego but you were the only choice from the hospital,' he said shortly. 'Your duties can be taken over by someone else—'

'And no one's indispensable,' she offered softly.

His shoulders lifted slightly in agreement. 'It wouldn't have been right to take one of the medical team away from their duties.'

She nodded, agreeing but none the less she was still hurt that she and her job were 'expendable'.

'Besides,' he went on, 'they say you're a workaholic, and though that is very admirable it isn't always a wise thing to make a life out of your work. You need some pleasure and leisure and I aim to give it to you.'

His words were almost a challenge, or, perhaps, a taunt; Sasha wasn't sure. In fact she was sure of nothing about him and it disturbed her greatly. If he thought that he was offering her the pleasure dome in the form of helping him out he was wrong. But he'd find that out soon enough. She closed the bedroom door on him.

'What's that smell?' Richard sniffed warily as he stepped out onto the veranda after sundown.

Sasha gave him a brief look of approval as she made the last adjustments to the table she had set for dinner. He was refreshed and wore white trousers and a burgundy-coloured silk shirt, open at the throat.

She too had made an effort to look nice for the evening, as she did every evening, not particularly for him. It was a ritual she enjoyed. It would have been so easy to be sloppy and uncaring in the heat-invasive Tropics but her upbringing was still important to her.

A soft breeze wafted the cerise silk of her sarong-style dress against her calves as she leaned over the table to light a candle in a glass bowl at the centre of the table.

'Patchouli, lemon grass and jasmine,' she told him.

'Some local dish, is it?'

Her soft laughter had him raising a surprised brow. 'Incense sticks,' she informed him. 'It's the only thing that keeps the mosquitoes at bay. I'm not sure which one they despise most so I burn all three to make sure. Does the smell offend you?'

'I'll get used to it.' He paused before going on. 'You are even more beautiful when you laugh. You should try it more often. Where shall I sit?'

The last question cushioned his compliment and Sasha felt that he had done it purposely, treading warily for fear of frightening her off, though frightening her off from what she didn't know.

Nodding towards the cane chair he was standing next to, she turned away to go back into the house for the food. Once inside she bit her lip. It was so long since a man had paid her a compliment, but pleasure didn't filter through her as it should have done, only an acute wariness.

Ruth would have seen Richard Carlton as a gift from the gods; Sasha only saw him as a threat to her future because of her past—a past that she had no need to feel shame for but one in which some sort of misplaced shame *had* been inflicted on her by his brother. Coupled as it was with her guilt for what she had done to the two families by running away, she had a lot to bear, and it would get more unbearable now that she was forced to spend time with Richard. He was a part of the past that she wanted zapped from her life.

'Can I help?'

Sasha jumped slightly, annoyed that her senses were suddenly so fragile, when he approached.

'Yes, please. Take these dishes out.' She handed him the bowl of salad and sweet potato and went to the oven for the fish she had baked with herbs and spices.

'I hope you like fish,' she said as they sat down to eat in the candlelight. 'It's more or less the staple diet out here.'

'Suits me.' He sampled it after she had dished it up and murmured his approval. 'I brought wine. It's in the fridge.'

If he expected her to get up and get it he had another think coming. 'I don't drink,' she told him, meeting his eyes across the table.

'Why?' He held hers as if it were the most important question in the world.

'I don't find it necessary.'

'You have nothing to escape from?'

Sasha held onto her senses because suddenly they were reeling. She didn't like that question; it was far too intrusive—as if he knew... But he couldn't because if he did he would have said so by now. Her reasoning only half worked. She thought that she would never be fully at ease with him.

'Is that why people drink—to escape?' she bravely asked.

'Some do. I don't. Join me?'

He got up and went into the bungalow for it without waiting for her agreement. She tried to relax. It was the only way. He had manipulated his way into her life and she was trapped. If they were to get on with each other she had to forget who he was and who she was and try not to think so suspiciously and negatively. He couldn't hurt her any more than she had been two years ago, and why should he want to anyway?

'It's not bad,' Sasha commented after taking a hesitant sip. 'Don't tell me you brought it all the way from New Zealand with you?'

'How did you know I was from New Zealand?'

'I don't,' she said quickly, and flicked the label of the wine bottle with her middle finger. 'The wine is, though.'

He nodded and smiled. 'I'm from Auckland; and you?'

To admit it would be a lesser evil than to deny it, she realised. She already had a new identity; creating a new birthplace for herself would be a further complication. Auckland was a big place.

'The same,' she murmured. Before he had time to get in another query she got in with her own. 'So tell me, why are you here?'

For the next half-hour as they ate and sipped their wine he outlined his quest for seeking suitable sites for hotels and tourist facilities on the islands.

Sasha had long since realised the importance of tourism and didn't make any comment to the contrary. Her two years here had opened her eyes; the people were poor and the adage about leaving the natives alone to live their lives in the age-old ways was nothing more than a romantic notion.

Prosperity brought better health and a better standard of living and, more importantly, it was what most of the Melanesians wanted. Sadly the earth's resources were dwindling at an alarming rate and it was getting more and more difficult to scratch a living from it.

The islanders craved videos and cars and fibreglass canoes, not the traditional dug-out pirogues of their forefathers. There would always be the carers who would safeguard their heritage but progress was inevitable. People like Richard Carlton were needed and wanted.

'Is that what you were doing in South America—investing in tourism?' she asked as she pushed the laden fruit bowl towards him.

He took a mango and squeezed it gently. His fingers were long and sensitive, and she wondered if they were like Geoff's because she couldn't recall Geoff's hands at all.

'No. Coffee, avocados and copper.'

Sasha smiled. 'Funny combination.'

'I bore easily,' he told her, with a small smile.

She tried to remember if she knew anything about him but came up with nothing but the fact that he wasn't very close to his family. Geoff was the blue-eyed boy of the Carltons—Daddy's boy, as Sasha had found.

'I brought coffee with me too. I'll make some.' He got up and went inside, and Sasha stretched and sat back, listening to the night sounds—the cicadas and the surf on the shore and the rustle of palm leaves a thousand miles up in the sky. She was relaxed and hadn't expected to be and the feeling was good.

Later, after their coffee, as she was clearing the table and Richard was wandering along the shoreline before bed, she paused to watch him, silhouetted against the sea and the sky by a moon as bright as a spotlight. He had wanted to wander alone, had actually said he'd prefer it if she didn't mind. She didn't mind, of course. She respected anyone who recognised that occasionally they needed their own space.

She watched and wondered about him and realised with that odd pull of her heart again that she was quite curious about him. She wondered about his relationship with Henrietta and why he had picked the Solomons to expand his horizons, and she was pleased to discover that all her wonderings were unconnected with her former fiancé.

Richard was Geoff's brother and they weren't a bit alike and in a way she was glad. If they were going to spend so much time together she would rather that he wasn't a constant reminder of the lucky escape she'd had two years ago.

But maybe that was asking too much of herself; maybe as they got to know each other better some of the Carlton characteristics would come through and she would despise him as much as she still despised Geoff.

He was still on the moon-bathed beach when she went to bed. She could see him through the protective mosquito mesh at her window. She wouldn't have minded him being here if he hadn't been a Carlton, she realised, but he was and she did mind, but there was nothing she could do about it except try and make as little pain for herself as possible. So far the only way to do that had been to try and forget who he was and who she was.

Sometimes she set herself some Herculean tasks, was her last thought as she drifted into a deep sleep.

CHAPTER FOUR

RICHARD was fixing the new generator when Sasha got up the next morning. She could hear him banging around in the lean-to at the back of the kitchen.

He'd had breakfast and left his dirty crockery in the sink and Sasha ignored it. She'd make it plain to him that he did his own clearing-up. She made her own breakfast—coffee and fruit—and then relented and washed the lot; after all, he was fixing her generator, wasn't he?

She took a coffee out to him.

'How did you sleep?' she asked, remembering her own first night on the island. Sleep had been out of the question as there were so many strange night noises to get used to—land crabs the size of footballs scurrying around under the bungalow, the squawking nocturnal bird life, the buzz of cicadas, snapping of dry foliage, the froth of the surf over the coral reefs—sounds she loved and found comforting now.

'Like the proverbial log,' he said, straightening up and taking the coffee from her outstretched hand.

'Wait till the rains and the cyclones come,' she teased.

'I'll be long gone by then.'

Sasha smiled to herself as she glanced up at the sky. The sun was shining now but clouds in the distance heralded rain later in the day. He'd learn soon enough that unpredictable was a fair description of the weather on this group of islands.

'Why the need for another generator?' he asked. 'You have two already.'

'One doesn't work at all and the solar doesn't after several days of cloud and rain. John said to order another and he'd pay. On reflection the new one is a wise investment, what with you and your video recorder.'

He stood drinking his coffee, watching her as she leaned against a post of the lean-to.

'What on earth brought you out here to this savage place?'

The question strengthened the thought that he didn't know all about her, but then he could be being tricky, trying to draw her out, trying to find out why she had jilted his brother before going in for the kill.

But no, she'd thought long and hard about all this in the early hours of the morning. She was going to give him the benefit of the doubt simply because a man like him had no reason to avenge his brother's jilting.

So, he'd asked a question and she was going to have to answer it. Lies she wasn't happy with, though that was hypocritical in the circumstances of her alternative identity—but that had been necessary. With him an adaptation of the truth was simpler, and it would save a lot of hassle and provide her with a very plausible excuse if he ever made a pass at her.

'Man trouble,' she told him. 'I had an unfortunate affair and decided that out was better than in.'

He nodded as if he understood. 'Married, was he?'

He asked so openly that it squashed any thought that he had any idea who the man in question was. Sasha was sure now that he knew nothing and she felt a calm relief which she knew would carry her through her time with him. It was going to be all right.

'No, he wasn't married. It just didn't work out and it was easier to go away than to stay.'

'Was it necessary to come quite so far?'

'Not really. The opportunity came up through a friend, and I had nothing to lose, so why not?'

She shrugged slightly, more to cover the shudder that threatened when she remembered what had led up to her coming here. She had been alone and virtually penniless in a downtown Singapore hotel when luck had at last shone her way. Betrayal had seemed to be her worst enemy at the time.

Her flight from New Zealand, while she was still dazed with shock over Geoff, had come about mainly because of her own stupidity and vulnerability. She hadn't been in her right mind at all.

In her horror at discovering the truth about the man she had been about to marry she had turned to an old friend of her father's—not a good friend, as she had soon found out. But at the time she had needed to lean on someone and Don Hertz had been there. He'd been leaving for Singapore on business and had suggested that she join him, and in her panic to get away, and blind to the truth of his intentions, she had foolishly agreed.

Don had been kind and sympathetic at first, but not so kind and sympathetic when he'd booked them into a hotel as man and wife. A man scorned was an ugly sight and once again Sasha had been forced to flee.

Two weeks alone and running out of money in a foreign city had been a salutary lesson and then, when despair had nearly forced her to back down and seek help from her family, she had met Christine.

Christine had had the room next to her and one night had knocked on Sasha's door asking for change for the television meter. She had turned out to be a good friend and had put her in touch with a worldwide agency that handled hospital staff. Within a week Sasha had been on her way to the Solomon Islands, no questions asked.

'And why not indeed?' Richard agreed softly. 'No regrets?'

She looked at him, slightly dazed, still reliving her traumatic experience. 'Regrets about what?' she asked.

'The job, the primitive lifestyle, the man you left behind?'

'No—no regrets,' she said staunchly.

'You sound very sure of that.'

'Why shouldn't I be? I love my job, and the primitive lifestyle has its compensations.' She smiled. 'There's nothing to live up to any more. As for the man—or any man come to that—I can live without him.'

'So you are wary of all men now, are you?' He held her eyes, perhaps seeking the truth before she had a chance to answer.

' "Wary" is an understatement,' she said lightly, and then added more firmly, ' "Immune" is probably the fitting word.'

He gave her a wry smile. 'That sounds like a warning.'

'It is,' she told him, and, heaving herself off the lean-to's post, she added with a touch of humour, 'A warning, not a challenge; remember that.'

'I will,' he murmured, and he sounded sincere. Sasha turned away and went back into the bungalow feeling that he had got the message, and she was glad.

'So what are your plans?' she asked him when he came into the kitchen later. She was at the sink, washing aubergines for lunch.

'Immediate plans are a swim and then to explore the hinterland. It will give me a fair idea of what to expect from the other islands I want to see. Will you join me?'

She was glad he had asked and not ordered as he mostly did, and she agreed.

She suggested that they take one of the canoes and swim from it further out to sea, beyond the reef, where the water was deeper and with any luck a school of dolphins would join them for some fun.

'Are you serious?' Richard asked as together they paddled out, not using the outboard being another of Sasha's suggestions. It was far too intrusive a sound and would have spoilt the tranquillity of the day.

'Of course,' she laughed. 'It's quite an experience— sort of magical. You'll see.'

Richard was first in the crystal-clear water, swimming strongly away from the canoe. Sasha watched him, her green eyes reflecting the intense green of the water. His body was powerful and deeply tanned and he moved as lithely as any creature of the sea. When he dived under the surface she held her breath with him till he emerged, shaking the water from his hair.

'It's spectacular down here—' He stopped, treading water as she held her index finger to her lips to silence him. He turned his head slightly and she heard a soft murmur of surprise come from his lips as the dolphins approached.

Silently Sasha slid over the edge of the canoe and into the warm water and slowly swam towards him. The dolphins, maybe a dozen of them, sleek and silvery, circled, curious and yet cautious. Sasha signalled to Richard to dive below the surface; she followed him down and they moved lazily under the water, giving the dolphins time to realise that they were not a threat.

The dolphins grew more confident and came closer, bringing their babies with them, showing them off proudly.

Sasha went up for air and Richard followed, and as they floated in the water the dolphins rocked and rolled all around them. Richard didn't speak, nor Sasha, and the only sound was of the gentle animals sighing and blowing and swishing the water as they frolicked.

Time stood still and the world didn't exist as again and again Sasha and Richard drew breath and went under to join the creatures in their play. All became more confident as a magical bond was formed between them.

One of the larger mothers nudged teasingly at Sasha and she reached out and stroked her neck, thrilling to the feel of the warm, silken flesh under her palms. The dolphin rolled over onto her back and then slid away as if beckoning her to follow.

Sasha surfaced, tiring now but reluctant to leave the beautiful creatures. She wondered what Richard was thinking and then knew that he must be as deeply affected by the experience as she. She had done this before, always alone, but this time was different, as if sharing the experience enhanced it. The dolphins were more playful, more friendly, somehow closer.

Sasha thought about it as she went down for the last time. It's because there are two of us, she mused. The dolphins saw them as a couple, paired off as nature intended humans and creatures to be.

As she blinked her eyes under the water she saw Richard with the young of the group, the nursery school, more lively and excitable than their elders, more daring.

Skittishly they spun around and under him, teasing him till he didn't know which way to turn.

For the last time Sasha surfaced; Richard followed and they swam leisurely back to the canoe, taking dragging breaths, with the dolphins gasping around them as if mimicking and gently mocking their lack of strength.

Exhausted, Sasha lay in the bottom of the boat, her head against the seat, her eyes closed against the glare of the sun, wanting to cherish the memory of swimming with the dolphins. She lay there as, the canoe rocking gently, Richard heaved himself in, and then the boat settled, and the gasping and the blowing of the dolphins receding into the distance were the only sound in the still, hot air.

And then a strange new languor spread like warm silk through her body as his mouth closed passionately over hers in a kiss so warm and erotically sensual that it would have been sacrilege to protest. It lingered tantalisingly till the silky, floaty feeling inside her billowed to an ache—an ache that dragged through her, pulling at the very last of her energy, leaving her dizzily weak.

When he drew back from her she blinked open her eyes and looked up into his, but she could barely focus on him for the sudden swelling of misty tears that clouded them.

'I'm sorry,' he breathed raggedly, and the apology came with such feeling that she didn't doubt that he genuinely did regret such a rash act. 'But that seemed the only thing to do after such a beautiful experience.'

He moved abruptly away from her to pick up a paddle, and Sasha didn't say a word as, bemused, she sat up and took hold of her own and used it automatically, not able to register what she was really doing.

No further word was spoken between them and there was no haste in their return to the shore. The only sounds were the slap of the paddles in the water, the shush of the surf and the thud as it broke on the beach.

In silence they dragged the canoe out of the water and in silence they walked slowly up the beach to the bungalow.

'I'll make the lunch,' he said when they reached the veranda.

Sasha just nodded, went into her bedroom and shut the door firmly behind her. Only when she had stripped off her bikini and stood in the small shower room that opened off her bedroom did she release the tension which was coiled nervously inside her. Leaning her forehead against the white tiles, she let out a small cry of dismay and anger, knowing that she couldn't be heard over the rush of the shower water.

That kiss had shaken her to her roots. It had been totally unexpected—so unexpected that she had been shocked into silence rather than shocked into a fury as she should have been. He'd apologised, though, and she could understand that he had been overwhelmed by the swim with the dolphins and so had done something he obviously hadn't planned.

She felt instinctively that it had been a rash action on his part—one he had regretted at the time. But perhaps he wasn't regretting it on reflection; perhaps he saw it as the open door to something more. Well, damn him, not if she could help it.

The only way to cope with it was to ignore it, forget it had ever happened. The trouble was that her lips still burned with that sweet pressure; like a firebrand it had scoured deep into her soft flesh and it would be a long time till that flesh had healed enough for her to forget that it had happened. Two years; and in that two years no one had kissed her that way—so sensually. Hell, no one had *ever* kissed her that way.

After sliding into shorts and a thin cotton shirt she went out onto the veranda where Richard was waiting for her. He'd changed into shorts and shirt and had prepared a light lunch of bread and cheese. As Sasha joined him at the table she prayed that he'd decided to ignore the impulse that had spurred the kiss and not mention it.

'As it's clouded over it might be a good idea to take a look at the rest of the island,' he suggested with little enthusiasm. 'I can't say trudging around under the glare of the sun appeals very much.'

Sasha's tension eased back. His tone was different, more guarded, as if he really did regret letting his reserve slide into that kiss.

'I'll take you to the jungle forest. You'll find it a sharp contrast after the dolphins.'

'In what way?'

'Wait and see.' She said it in a teasing way and forced a teasing smile to go with it, and he smiled and visibly relaxed, as if he had been expecting her to bring up the subject of the kiss and was relieved that she hadn't.

'I've seen a rainforest before, you know. South America isn't exactly short of them.'

'Ah, but you haven't seen one like this. It has hidden secrets.'

'Such as?'

'*Wait and see*,' she repeated.

* * *

'The island is boot-shaped. I call it Mini Italy. Talking of boots, I'm glad to see you've got some,' she said later as they were getting ready to set off.

'I did my homework before setting out on this trip. I think I've got just about everything to cover every eventuality.'

'I didn't see any oilskins amongst your belongings,' she goaded, with mischief in her eyes.

'Ah, you've got me there. No oilskins. Will I need them?'

Sasha nodded, and with a smile she handed him Ruth's cape from the hook on the porch. 'In approximately twenty minutes' time we are going to be deluged. Remember to put your oilskin on *before* you get soaked otherwise you'll be incubating your own sauna.'

''Struth,' he laughed. 'You're a mine of good advice.'

'I've learnt the hard way,' she told him, picking up her rucksack and heaving it around her shoulders.

He swung his camera equipment across his shoulders, and as they headed up along a narrow path behind the bungalow he said, 'You surprise me, you know—a well-educated girl from Auckland adapting to this steamy life on the islands. It's quite a revelation.'

It was there again, that feeling that he knew everything about her.

'How do you know I'm well educated?' she asked, trying to make it sound like a casual question.

'Accent and occupation. Was it hard to adapt?'

I'm getting paranoid, Sasha thought. This is nothing but a normal conversation between two people getting to know each other. 'It was a bit, I suppose,' she admitted. 'It was more of a cultural jolt than anything. Some of the islands were a terrible shock to the system for someone who had grown up with an inside loo,' she joked, trying to ease her own tension.

She walked on ahead as the track grew too narrow for them to walk side by side. She knew the track and he didn't object, and she reflected that when he allowed that damned reserve of his to drop he was quite human. In fact he was quite an easygoing sort of man when you got to know him.

As predicted, the rain started twenty minutes to the minute after they had set off, and they paused under the shade of a tree to put on their oilskins. The heat was oppressive as the first huge drops fell, but Sasha knew that once the rain set in the temperature could drop rapidly.

'Perhaps this wasn't such a good idea,' Richard said with concern as the track beneath their feet quickly became a greasy mêlée of rainwater washing over mud and forest debris.

'And they call this paradise,' Sasha called out over the rush of water from the heavens. 'Are you sure you want to develop these islands for tourism?'

'Positive,' was all he said as they battled their way on, climbing upwards and into deeper undergrowth.

After a while the incline levelled out but it was still hard going. The ground was spongy and dangerously uneven, roots from trees crawling on the surface a constant hazard, the cloying thickness of ferns and shrubs a threat to what they might conceal. On her first venture here Sasha had been terrified of snakes and creepy-crawlies but had soon realised that she was a bigger threat to them.

'Nearly there,' she called out.

'Nearly where? The Suya Hilton, I hope.'

Sasha turned and laughed because he didn't often make jokes. At that moment of turning she missed her footing. She fell clumsily, landing flat on her face in warm, sticky mud.

He had her in his arms in an instant, up and out of the quagmire at her feet, lifted up as if she had been a small child. Their oilskins squeaked together at the unceremonious contact.

Sasha clutched at him to keep her balance and he held her tightly as she shook the water and mud from her face and caught her breath. And then she caught her breath again at the expression on his face—a mixture of concern for her and a sort of confusion, and then a darkening of his eyes as if he was cross with her for falling.

'Are you all right?' He shook her slightly.

She nodded, spluttering a mouthful of grit from her lips.

His hand came up from under his oilskin and smoothed the mud from her lips and chin and Sasha felt the contact through the whole of her body. Shocked as she was after her tumble, she recognised the shot of awareness of him and recoiled from it so sharply that he nearly lost his footing.

'I...I'm sorry...I'm OK...just annoyed with myself for being so...so careless,' she croaked, trying to smooth down her oilskin which suddenly felt so weighty and uncomfortable that she wanted to fling it off.

'Here, let me take your rucksack; it's too much for you,' he said impatiently.

'No! I'm OK!' she insisted. 'We'll go on—'

'No, we'll go back. We shouldn't have come out in this nonsense weather.'

'Well, we'll get nowhere in that case; most of the weather is nonsense here,' Sasha insisted. 'We're nearly there anyway.'

He backed down. 'I hope this secret place of yours is worth it.'

This time he took the lead, picking his way through the undergrowth, making sure that the terrain was safe for her. So he had some consideration, she thought, and she was touched, but only mildly. He had shaken her like a rag doll back there, obviously cross with her for being a woman.

'Over to the left,' she called out, and he followed her direction.

In the time she had been here she had beaten a path to her secret place, but the rate of growth of the vegetation, accelerated by the heavy rainfall and the cloying humidity, was hard to keep up with. The track was barely visible now.

Richard stopped suddenly and she knew that he had seen it—the grim outline of a past that was almost too terrible to contemplate unless you knew the truth, which Sasha did.

She sloshed through the mud to stand by his side. Neither spoke for a long time.

The silence around them was profound—broken only by the plop and shush of the rain filtering down through the forest around and above them, whichever way they turned.

The rusting bulk of a war plane lay cushioned in the dank forest as if it had dropped there only days ago. One wing was severed from the body like a chicken wing torn from a carcass and lay a few yards away in the undergrowth, almost enveloped by a matted tangle of shrubbery. The other wing was still attached but bent and mangled and badly rusted by the savagery of a thousand storms and cyclones over the years.

Beyond the wreck, in sharp contrast to the emotive sight, was a still pool of black water, so serene, so exotically beautiful that it took your breath away. It was surrounded by dripping orchids and ferns and flora so lush and green that it was hard to imagine that such a spectacle could be witnessed alongside the wreckage of a war plane that had been shot down in a brutal battle long ago.

'Shelter,' Sasha murmured, and stepped past him to push aside a curtain of clinging green tendrils that hung down over the gaping side of the hulk. She climbed into the rusted cabin and turned to him.

'It's safe; no ghosts.'

He frowned, raked his hand uncertainly through his sopping wet hair, and then climbed in beside her.

'It's long since been stripped,' she told him. 'Anything of worth was snaffled years ago for souvenirs.'

She shrugged off her oilskin cape and the rucksack and let them drop to the floor of the hot cabin. Richard stood transfixed for a moment and then did the same, but took more care with his camera equipment.

'So this is your secret place,' he said, unimpressed. 'Don't you find it spooky?' he added, disdainfully sniffing the fusty atmosphere.

Sasha laughed lightly and, stooping slightly, she went to the front of the cabin and scooped aside a curtain of greenery growing over the open windscreen, the glass from which had long since been hauled away for some purpose one couldn't imagine.

'How can it be spooky when you look out on that?'

The black pool with its ring of exotica was directly in front of them. A mist of rain swirled over it now but the colours of the flowers and orchids around it were still vibrant, with an elusive mystery to them.

'How could anything so lovely survive the dank depths of the perpetually wet forest?' she mused softly. She turned to him and smiled hesitantly, not sure if he would understand what she got out of this place. 'I like to think that when this plane came down during World War II that was the first sight the airmen saw. They must have thought themselves in paradise.'

Richard gazed at her for a second and then slumped down on one of the metal seats that ran along the side of the cabin. 'Or heaven,' he suggested ruefully.

Sasha sat across from him and took water and some biscuits out of her rucksack, and a towel to dry her hair. She understood what must be going through his mind. She poured some water into a plastic cup and handed it to him.

'No heaven, no hell, no ghosts because no one died here,' she told him.

'I think that highly improbable,' Richard said sombrely, taking the water from her. 'The battle of Guadalcanal was brutal. Thousands died here— Japanese and Americans—'

'I know,' Sasha interrupted excitedly, eager to tell him what she knew. 'The islands and the waters here are littered with wrecks. But these boys didn't die. The day they came down a small miracle happened for them.'

He laughed uncertainly and shook his head slightly as if he didn't believe her.

'It's true,' she insisted, leaning forward to stress her point. 'I know.'

His eyes met hers across the shady interior of their temporary shelter—teasing eyes, disbelieving eyes. 'Don't tell me you have psychic powers?'

'No, just an inquisitive mind,' she told him, with a secretive smile. 'I checked, you see.'

'Checked? What do you mean you checked?'

She leaned back against the side of the plane and sipped some water. 'When I first came here I was struck by the tragedy of it all, thinking how futile it all was— you know, war. I sat in here and looked out at the pool and tried to imagine what it was like all those years ago. You can't, of course; you can't ever imagine what went on. It was a different generation, different times.

'But the longer I sat here, the more I got the feeling that this was a good place and not a bad one. I wanted to believe that those men came out of it alive. I wanted to believe it so much that I wanted to find out. There was a number and some letters on the side of the plane, another group of numbers etched on what was once the instrument panel. I checked them out.'

'Are you kidding?' Richard asked in disbelief.

Sasha laughed at the astonished expression on his face. 'No, I'm deadly serious. It took an age—months and months of enquiries and dead ends. Eventually, through a contact in Honiara, I got in touch with a war historian in America who did the work for me.

'This plane we are sheltering in came down in January 1943. There were four reconnaissance airmen aboard, all boys of about my age—twenty-three. All escaped serious injury due to the skill of the pilot who brought them down. An American warship saw them hit the forest and sent out a launch to pick them up. A month later the battle was over.'

'And they all lived happily ever after.' His tone wasn't devoid of cynicism.

'I like to think so,' Sasha murmured. 'I like to think they got back to the States and married, if they weren't already, and had children and their children had children. It's nice to think that their great-grandchildren are probably going to school at this very moment.'

'You surprise me,' he said after a long pause. 'You're quite a romantic at heart.'

She was a romantic at heart—no, she had been, till life had disillusioned her. She took a breath.

'I made this my secret place because I wanted something nice to believe in. When I sit here I don't think about anything other than the good that came out of a potentially hopeless situation.'

'That sounds very profound.'

'Not really. I'm sure you must have a secret place you can gather your thoughts in.'

'I've never really thought about it,' he mused. 'I suppose my secret place is my head.'

Sasha laughed. 'Only a man could say that.'

He smiled ruefully. 'Men aren't romantic like women.'

'More's the pity. Have a biscuit.' She offered him the packet and widened her eyes in surprise as he burst out laughing.

'What's so funny?'

'Well, offering me a biscuit after lamenting the lack of romance in men wasn't a particularly romantic thing to do.'

The smile slid from Sasha's mouth and a pulse throbbed dully at her throat. A small trickle of perspiration irritated her neck and she scrubbed it away with the tips of her fingers.

'I wasn't aware that this was a romantic situation,' she said tightly.

'But we were talking of romance,' he said softly.

'You brought it up!'

He eyed her curiously, and then said in a voice that seemed to grate right through her, 'He must have hurt you very badly for you to be so wary of men.'

For a long time Sasha sat in silence, staring down at the corroded floor of the plane. She wished she'd never brought him here. Why had she? She'd brought no one here before, so why him?

'Yes, he hurt me very badly,' she admitted at last, her voice only a whisper in the soporific heat of their enclosure. The rush of rain outside had eased and was a gentle shush now. She could almost hear her own heart beating inside her, thudding and thudding in rage at all that this man's brother had done to her.

Yes, she'd been hurt, but not in the way he thought. Geoff's betrayal had injured her pride more than her heart. She had realised very soon after fleeing to Singapore that her heart wasn't aching for the loss of a love but because of the horror of his betrayal and the fact that he had only wanted to marry her because his father needed the merger of the two families. Geoff had left her with such a wariness of being cheated that she wouldn't allow anyone into her heart ever again.

She stood up and started to pack away the bottle of water and the biscuits. Her fingers trembled as she worked but her body shielded them from him. 'We'd better get back.'

'I want to take some pictures first.'

She reached down for her oilskin; he helped her pull it over her head and she wasn't quick enough to avoid the contact of his fingers on the back of her neck. For some reason her heart squeezed and she went to turn away, but he grasped at her shoulders and made her look at him.

When he spoke his voice was low and throaty. 'I'm not sorry for kissing you this morning, though I did apologise at the time. I want to do it again. Given the right circumstances, I might want more than a kiss, though. How do you feel about that?'

She stared up at him, shocked rigid by what he was suggesting. Her mind raced although her body was incapable of moving out of his grasp. She ran her tongue nervously over her lips and then spoke, coldly and flatly.

'I don't feel anything, Richard Carlton, not for you or your suggestion. I've told you, I'm not wary of men, simply immune to them. I'm not nursing a broken heart for a lost lover, I'm nursing a bruised ego for a wicked betrayal. I don't want you and I don't need you—'

'And a philosophy like that, as you probably well know, smacks of a challenge that every red-blooded male would take up.'

Suddenly he let her go. 'Except me,' he added brutally, his eyes dark with an anger she didn't understand. 'I don't have to chase women. Women usually chase me. So you can forget your mystical cavorting with the dolphins, your little secret places for meditation, your little challenges thrown out under cover of a bruised ego—they don't wash with me.'

With that he turned and leapt out of the plane, snatching his camera equipment as he went.

Sasha stood in the doorway in a fury of temper at his damned, damned arrogance. He actually thought that she fancied him and was playing some sort of tricky game with him!

As he sloshed over to the still, black pool, swiping at branches and leaves as he went, she shouted out fiercely, 'I didn't take you swimming or bring you here because I want you to take up some sort of challenge. If you think I lust after your body you're very much mistaken! It falls very short of my needs, I promise you. Damn you, just damn you and your fat ego!'

Grabbing her rucksack, she leapt down from the plane and, slithering and panting, headed back the way they'd come, hoping that he would get lost without her, or get bitten to death by mosquitoes, or fall in the pool, or get savaged by a wild pig in the forest. How could he, how *could* he have spoiled it all?

It was only later, as she saw the reeded roof of the bungalow through the trees below her, that her rage abated and she gave serious thought to why she had taken him out with the dolphins and taken him to her secret place in the forest. She'd done it because for the first time in two years she had wanted to share something with someone.

Yes, she realised with a sinking heart, she'd wanted to share it. But what deeply puzzled her was why she had chosen to share it with him of all people. Why damned, pushy Richard Carlton?

CHAPTER FIVE

SASHA was up early the next morning, starving because she hadn't eaten the night before. She'd shut herself in her bedroom all night, suffering the heat, feeling a prisoner in her own home. She'd heard him fooling around with the radio, clattering around in the kitchen, scraping about on the veranda till the early hours of the morning. She had fumed in her room, honestly expecting him to knock and apologise, but he hadn't.

And the wretched rain had driven on and on, pressing the heat down on the roof till the pressure was in her own head. Well, it had to stop—the pressure, the aggro from him. He'd have to go or she would. She'd tell him. Just as soon as he showed his face she'd tell him.

She ate a mango and biscuits for breakfast and drank two cups of coffee on the veranda steps before he emerged from his room, looking shaved and refreshed. The sun came out with him and Sasha cynically thought that whoever had said that the sun shone on the righteous had never met Richard Carlton.

'When you're ready we'll pack up, take a couple of canoes and spend a few days touring some of the other islands.'

Sasha opened her mouth to protest but he'd gone back inside. He returned almost immediately with a cup, poured himself a coffee and sat on the veranda above her to drink it.

She turned her back to him and stared out to sea. 'I'm not going on any tours with—'

'Don't be silly, Sasha,' he interrupted wearily, as if he'd anticipated her reaction before he'd made the suggestion.

'I'm not being silly. I'm being quite reasonable—so reasonable that I didn't throw you out last night as I should have done. I waited till the morning, you see. I'm throwing you out now.' He didn't say a word and she turned to see him watching her. 'Did you hear what I said?'

'Yes, and I'm not going and neither are you, so stop being female and let's discuss what we ought to take with us to make our trip easier.' His eyes were deadly serious as he spoke but it didn't put Sasha off.

'How many times do I have to repeat myself? I'm—'

'And how many times do I have to repeat *my*self?' he echoed sharply. 'Listen, sweetheart, we are in this together because that's the way it is.'

'Because if I pull out you'll do your utmost to see I don't work on these islands any more?' she argued, guessing his intentions.

'I wouldn't lower myself to make such a threat.'

'You'd do it, though!'

'I won't have to. You mess up my plans and someone else will do it for me.'

'The Hun of course,' Sasha blurted out hotly. 'I'm certainly adept at picking my enemies, aren't I?'

He gave her a small, arrogant smile. 'You are rather, but I didn't have Henrietta in mind, though she'd be sure to put her oar in if your future was at stake. No, Sasha, her uncle would not take kindly to you being the cause of me pulling my finances out of the islands. He needs me as much as I need you, and if you break the circle and pull out you'll be the first for the chop.'

'I'll take that chance—'

'Don't take it, Sasha,' he warned gravely. 'I know John Harvey; he's a generous man where the hospital is concerned, but when the money dries up you might not find him quite so benevolent.'

'And what exactly do you mean by that?'

'I mean that if he doesn't start raking in some money soon there won't be any left for those generous grants of his to the hospital.'

She widened her eyes. 'John has—money problems?' she breathed haltingly.

'His benevolence isn't a bottomless pit. He's made some bad investments lately and needs a top-up. If I agree to invest in these islands he'll be in for a hefty rake-off.'

'And the hospital will live,' Sasha stated ruefully. 'If that isn't emotional blackmail I don't know what is.'

'That's the way it is in business—always someone scratching someone's back. It's not really an issue, Sasha, but you're making it one.'

'Because I'm the one victimised in all this. Do as you're told, Sasha, or else!'

Richard gave out a deep sigh. 'I really don't see what the problem is. A few weeks hacking around the islands with me, barbecues on the beaches, swimming with the dolphins—'

'And putting up with you touching me, insulting me with your suggestions—'

'You really are making heavy weather of all this.'

Sasha's green eyes narrowed and her lips tightened. 'No, Richard, *you* are. We're only just into it and—'

'I kissed you. Is it such a big thing?'

It had been to her—an enormous affront to her privacy—but obviously it had meant nothing to him. He probably kissed women all the time and thought nothing of it.

'I expect it's a pretty big thing to Henrietta,' she suggested, eyeing him curiously, wondering again how deep their relationship was.

'Do you mean me kissing you or me kissing Henrietta?'

Sasha sighed and turned away from him, gazed out to sea and wished this conversation weren't taking place and that she were here alone with her thoughts. But she wasn't; he was here in all his glory and making life difficult for her. Or was she making it difficult for herself?

'Is Henrietta a problem for you?' he asked quietly.

Just one hint of mocking and she would have fled, but his question had been asked with concern and that was his saviour. She swivelled round and faced him again.

'No, she isn't a problem for me. I know what you're thinking—that I believe you shouldn't have kissed me if you're having a meaningful relationship with her. But frankly I don't care about the kiss and I don't care if you are on the brink of marriage to her—something that I'm sure would be a good business relationship for you and her uncle because I get the distinct impression that there isn't much love lost between you—but what I really object to is being accused of playing games.'

He made no apology and really she hadn't expected one because he probably saw no wrong in what he'd said.

She got up from the steps and went and stood by him at the veranda table.

Softly she said, 'I had no ulterior motive for sharing either the dolphins or my secret place in the rainforest with you. I just judged you to be a person who might appreciate the experiences for what they were worth in this grotty world. I was mistaken. Bad judgement on my part—nothing else, I assure you. If you see it as something else then that is your problem, not mine. My conscience is clear.'

She lifted the tray of coffee and carried it back into the bungalow, leaving him sitting there.

She was drying up when he wandered into the kitchen. He stood watching her for a few minutes. She felt acutely uncomfortable under his perusal but said nothing because she'd said enough. At last he spoke.

'I owe you an apology,' he said quietly. 'My only excuse is that I didn't realise how sensitive you were. It does nothing for my ego when you freeze if I touch you. No woman has frozen under my touch before.'

Sasha couldn't help a wry smile. 'That's some ego you have to live with. I feel sorry for you, having got to your age without experiencing rejection. It's character-building. I know.'

'You didn't reject me when I kissed you in the canoe.'

Sasha raised her eyes skyward and let out a small laugh of derision. 'I didn't shout whoopee either.' She looked at him. 'I didn't slap you down in the canoe because for one thing you took me completely by surprise, and for another I didn't want to spoil what we had just been through with the dolphins. I *suffered* that kiss.' She shrugged. 'It didn't mean anything to me.'

'Well, I think it did,' he said bluntly. 'I think you thought it a fitting conclusion to the experience as well.'

Deep in her heart Sasha finally had to admit that it was true. It had been a beautiful kiss, but a dangerous one. She hadn't thrilled to the danger of it.

'But you believed that I was open to something more.'

'It's usually the prelude to something more between consenting adults.'

'But *I'm* not a consenting adult.'

'That's why I asked what you thought instead of taking what I wanted. Perhaps you would have preferred the other way—brute force and ask questions after or, worse, no questions asked.'

Sasha shook her head in incredulity. 'Your chat-up line is beyond belief. What's the success rate? Nought out of a thousand, I'd say.'

He smiled cynically. 'I haven't got to a thousand yet.'

'But getting warm, no doubt,' she retorted scathingly, moving him aside to put the spoons away.

'Am I getting warm with you or are you playing games, warming me up for the big rejection?'

The way he said that made her think that he was referring to his brother's rejection. Her eyes widened fearfully and searched his for the truth. Was he making veiled suggestions to try and unnerve her? Oh, God, she couldn't read him; it was hopeless.

'No chance of getting anywhere warm with me,' she bit out icily.

'What would it take to defrost you, Sasha? Your lost lover back in your arms? He must have been one hell of a guy.'

She looked at him painfully, wondering if she had imagined a hint of regret in his voice, as if he was hurt that she was so immune to him. No, his ego was bruised, that was all.

'He was one hell of a bastard if you must know,' she told him with feeling.

'And yet you loved him and still do,' he probed.

Sasha steeled herself. Probing from him of all people was the last thing she wanted. She was talking about his evil brother here, and yet if he knew that surely he would come to his defence in some way? He couldn't know; she willed that to be the case more strongly than ever.

'I *think* I loved him *before* I found out he was a hell of a bastard. End of story. I'm not carrying any emotional baggage, whatever you might think.'

She lifted her chin defiantly, wanting to change the subject and for some reason wanting to get back at him. 'Talking of baggage, what exactly *is* your relationship with Henrietta?' Actually she had no interest whatsoever in his love life, but since he seemed intent on drawing out her reasons for living then why not have a stab at drawing out his?

He smiled somewhat wearily. 'My relationship with Henrietta has more of a meaningless nature than a meaningful one. And, before you ask the next inevitable question, no, I've never been in love, and the thought of being so has palled after what I've seen my brother put through. He was jilted on the eve of his wedding and it wasn't a pleasant experience for anyone.'

Sasha opened her mouth to protest, to defend herself somehow and say it hadn't damned well been a pleasant experience for herself either, but she clamped her mouth shut again. How could she do that without revealing all? She had held back then and she would have to hold back now, and sometimes this holding back made it all so much worse. Would she ever be able to give her side of the story?

Not with him, she thought in resignation; not with Geoff's brother. And yet, if she wanted to confess, Richard Carlton was the one she wanted to confide in and she really didn't understand her reasoning on that one.

'So where do we go from here?' he said, slicing into her thoughts.

So he was as evasive about love and women as she was about men. They should have made an ideal couple, she mused wryly.

'If we could keep this trip of yours on an impersonal level it might be all right,' she suggested bluntly.

'But you suspect that we can't?' he suggested.

'I suspect that *you* can't.'

She hated it when she had to wait for his reply. He did it on purpose to prolong her agony. He smiled when he did it, too, as if he knew something she didn't. It irritated her.

'I find you interesting and fanciable, and I'd be a liar if I said I didn't want to pursue the relationship to a deeper plane,' he said at last.

'You haven't got a deeper plane,' she retorted angrily. 'You said it yourself—the idea of love has palled for you, but you wouldn't discourage me from sharing your bed, would you? Is that what you mean by a deeper plane?'

He held his hands up in mock defence of himself. 'I'm backing off because this is getting too deep for me. I want the job done with the minimum of trouble. I put my work before anything else.'

'So I'm "anything else", am I?' She couldn't help the disgruntled tone in her voice. He'd tried it on with her for no other reason than that she was there to be tried on. She shouldn't have been stung by that because she wasn't in the least bit interested in him, but it just added to what she thought of men in general: they were users.

'No, you're not "anything else". You're a very lovely lady with a mega chip on your shoulder where men are concerned and—'

'And you think you might be able to help?' she said with cynicism.

'I think it would be a waste of a beautiful life to live with that chip for too long.'

'I think you presume far too much, Richard, but thanks for your concern anyway.'

She draped the teatowel over the top of the cooker, trying to appear nonchalant, as if his concern didn't matter to her in the least. Secretly it did. It worried her deeply. She didn't want anyone getting into her secret self, especially not him. It occurred to her that she might not have been quite so prickly if he hadn't been Geoff's brother, but then that was almost an admission that she found him attractive and was thawing, and she wasn't.

'So, plans; we ought to make some, and conditions,' she went on in a businesslike tone.

'Ah, conditions. Surprise me.'

'You know the conditions. Lay off the personal issues.'

'Keep my hands off you?'

'Yes, and the rest. Familiarity breeds contempt. If you still want me to show you round the islands let's keep our conversations on a business level.' She folded her arms across her chest and waited for his response to that.

He looked doubtful, pursing his lips as if he was considering it but not getting very far—those lips that had invaded hers so sensuously. Sasha inwardly rebelled against thinking of his lips that way but there was nothing she could do about it.

'You're asking an awful lot, you know. We'll be spending every minute together, more than likely sleeping together—'

Sasha's blood surged at the thought. 'Just a minute; how come we are suddenly potential sleeping partners?'

He gave a small shrug. 'Some of the islands I want to see are uninhabited. We'll have to make our own shelter for the nights; sleeping together under the same palm-frond roof will be far more practical than wasting time making two.'

Their living requirements hadn't crossed her mind. In fact when it came down to the fundamentals she hadn't given the trip any serious thought at all. She only knew of three islands in close proximity that were actually inhabited; certainly none of them had hotels. And they would need shelter against the rains and the mosquitoes and whatever else these savage isles could throw at them.

'OK, so we have to share a roof—'

'We'll have to share a great deal more than just a roof, Sasha. We'll be living in each other's pockets.' She looked alarmed at that and Richard went on, 'The point I'm trying to make is that if we're not careful we could...'

He paused, fixing his eyes on her intently—so intently that she felt prickles down her spine. She vaguely wondered about her spine. She'd never had any problems with it before but since his invasion of her life it seemed to have become the barometer of her emotions.

'We could what?' she urged, eager to escape that penetrating gaze of his.

'We could easily do something we might regret, like falling into that deeper plane.'

'Falling into bed, you mean?' She laughed lightly to perish the thought. 'By the time you rig up our shelter for the night, Richard "Tarzan" Carlton, passion will be the last thing on your mind!'

'And your passion?' he teased.

'It doesn't exist,' she told him haughtily. 'I thought you already knew that.'

He held her insolent gaze for a long while and then, as if the conversation had never taken place, he said, 'Maps. I'll get them while you brew another pot of coffee. I've already made a provisional list of what we need to take with us and...'

Sasha didn't hear any more. In a stupor she turned to the coffee, only vaguely aware that he had left the kitchen. Their conversation had upset her more than she had shown.

He was immune to love and so was she. Fair enough, but it posed a lot of worrisome thoughts about the future. It was nothing to do with him, though he had sown the seeds of her disquiet by mentioning it. Would she spend the rest of her life celibate and alone, without a partner, without a lover?

She made the coffee and tried to push the thought to the very back of her mind. It wasn't worth thinking about.

They left after lunch with two canoes packed tight with supplies and Richard's equipment. He intended videoing places that seemed hopeful for development and had ringed them on his map. Not wishing to put a dampener on his plans, Sasha only vaguely hinted that some of the islands he wanted a closer look at would probably be a disappointment to him, but he was not to be dissuaded from his intention of seeing it all, good and bad.

Their first stop was an island that was a true paradise, too small for a community to live off but only a few miles from a bigger island, which was in fact so big that there was a clinic, a small outpost of the main hospital in Kula, and a thriving population of several hundred Melanesians.

'We'll make camp here for the night and go on first thing in the morning,' he told her after cutting the outboard engine.

They were towing the second canoe to save on fuel. It took a lot of time and effort to get both craft beached, and once they were safely out of the water they both headed for the shade of the palm trees and flopped, exhausted and hot, onto the soft sand.

'Listen to that silence,' Richard murmured after a while.

'If you listen intently enough you can hear a thousand sounds,' she murmured back, her eyes closed, her breathing gradually becoming regular again.

'Name them.'

'Palm-fronds shushing in the breeze, the lap of surf on the shore, crickets back in the scrub there.' She paused, listening for more sounds she could identify.

'That's three; only nine hundred and ninety-seven to go.'

Suddenly there was a dull thud only a few feet away from them. Sasha blinked open her eyes.

'What the devil was that?'

She eased up onto her elbows and smiled. 'It sounded like manna from heaven to me. Only nine hundred and ninety-six to go.' She nodded towards a coconut that had just dropped from the tree above them, landing a few feet away in the sand. 'If you've the energy to go down to the canoes for the machete we can quench our thirst,' she suggested, getting up on her knees to collect the coconut.

He didn't need any further encouragement to stride off down the beach. Sasha sat back against the trunk of the palm, cradling the coconut in her hands while she waited. She watched him searching in the canoe for the large knife and wondered at him. Here was a man, abundant with wealth, acting like some modern-day Robinson Crusoe.

He came back with the machete, and with a grin she handed him the coconut. She doubted if he had any idea what to do with it.

'Hit it,' she urged.

'Obviously,' he murmured. 'If I miss have you the wherewithal to stitch me up?'

'I could if I had to. I've seen it done once or twice. You'd be the first, though.'

'In that case I won't take any chances.' He aimed accurately and Sasha winced, and when she opened her eyes he was holding out a dripping husk to her. She quenched her thirst with the sweet, milky fluid and handed him the rest.

He sat down beside her and drank.

'Was that your first time?' she asked, secretly admiring him for swiping at the coconut so accurately.

'The coconut?'

She gave him a look and he half smiled. 'Yes, the first. My privileged upbringing and lifestyle didn't take into account knocking the heads off coconuts and drinking the contents. So what shall we do for supper, or is that it?' He poked at the coconut with a brittle palm-frond he'd picked up from the hot sand.

Sasha scrambled to her feet. 'I'll fish if you want to build a fire—if you know *how* to build a fire,' she couldn't resist adding.

He gave her an old-fashioned look and got to his feet. 'Good idea; you fish and I'll do what a man has to do— build some sort of shelter for the night.'

She watched him crashing through the cloying undergrowth, a powerful man with broad shoulders and muscled legs, tanned and athletic, with dark hair curling at the nape of his neck. She felt a shiver down her spine again, and with a dismissive shrug she turned to go down to the canoes to unpack what they might need for the night.

Damn him, he'd probably have built a two-storey dwelling with a roof garden by the time she got back. The fish had better bite or she'd be in trouble.

'That's incredible,' Sasha enthused later. She'd been watching him on and off from the canoe that she had unloaded and taken out into a small bay to fish for their supper, wondering how he was doing.

'Well, it isn't the Savoy,' he said, reminding her of an earlier conversation, 'but it will do.'

He'd stripped off his T-shirt and was slicked with perspiration from his efforts. He'd built a shelter out of palm leaves and huge ferns found in the jungle—a shelter with a thick, impenetrable roof and three sides, but open at the front. It faced the sea but was sheltered by a crop of palms. It was an incredible effort for a man of his 'privileged upbringing'.

'Do you think it will hold up if it rains?' she asked.

'Will it rain? You're the authority on the weather.'

Sasha shrugged. 'I only know the idiosyncrasies of my own island.' She glanced up at the sky and then at the horizon where already the sun was dipping threateningly below it. The sky was clear. 'I hope not.'

'We've always got the tent to fall back on if it does.' He turned to her. 'Any luck, or is barbecued coconut on the menu?' He whistled on sight of her catch in a net at her feet. 'We'll feast like kings. Am I permitted a shower before we get the fire going?'

Her eyes widened. 'You haven't fixed up an *en-suite* bathroom as well?'

'The sea.' He grinned and, taking a towel from the pile of stuff she'd unloaded, flung it over his shoulder and went down the beach.

Sasha gathered driftwood for the fire, taking suspicious glances at the palm-frond shelter he had built. It wasn't over-spacious and they would be sleeping there together tonight. She could hardly refuse to share it with him after all his efforts, and she'd be unwise to anyway for many reasons—mosquitoes for one.

She'd sensibly brought nets with them and they could be draped over the front, cocooning them in safety... cocooning them together under a starry sky, close together in the heat of the night. She shivered though the heat was stifling. She couldn't do it... she'd suggest the tent...

Her heart stilled as she threw the driftwood down in a heap and sank down beside it to build it into a fire.

It wasn't a problem and she wasn't going to make one out of it. She'd made it plain that she wanted nothing to do with him in that way and he had accepted that. After this morning the rest of the day had been a pleasant relief. They seemed to be getting along just fine.

So why was her heart thudding again as he came up the beach, towelling his wet hair, striding masterfully towards her like some Greek god? She shivered again, not knowing why, but suffering it because it was happening and she couldn't stop it.

Together they grilled the fish on sticks over the fire, and then Sasha pushed green bananas in their skins in the ashes to bake. Richard had found nuts and pawpaws and they drank wine, their only concession to civilisation and the only bottle that Richard had brought with them. It was a banquet under the stars, with the scene before them, the velvet sky and the moon dancing off the black satin sea, a truly beautiful sight.

Richard sat with his arms around his knees, cradling a plastic cup of wine in his fingers. Sasha leaned back against a palm, scarcely able to keep her eyes open.

'I've been rattling round the world making money for so long that I've tended to overlook the simple pleasures of life.' He turned to her. 'You've found it, haven't you?'

'What, the Holy Grail?' she murmured sleepily. She could see his smile in the glow of what remained of the fire.

'You've adapted, found a new life for yourself. Here you are, a girl from Auckland who's shunned the good life for a simpler one. I've watched you today, taking everything in your stride, fishing out there in a canoe you paddled out yourself, cooking this meal without squealing in horror at the primitive fare. A hundred times

I've put Henrietta in your place and imagined how she would react.'

'I don't think it takes much of an imagination to see how she would react. She wouldn't even have set foot on this island without the red carpet being laid out for her.'

'Even then she wouldn't.' He smiled. 'Are you happy with your life, Sasha?'

The question nudged at her languid weariness. It was so pointed and it made her reflect on what he had said before about her finding a new life for herself. Had she said she'd done that—shunned a good life for a simpler one? Her head felt so heavy with the wine and the day's exertions that she could hardly think. But the question thudded dully through her fatigue. Was she happy?

Richard didn't prompt her for an answer; he gazed at her for a while as if making up his own mind. Sasha couldn't meet his look, and couldn't answer him either because suddenly she felt a deep pain of awareness inside her, a terrible realisation that she wasn't happy. Contented maybe, fulfilled in her work, but happy? She'd thought she was, she'd never considered that she wasn't, but now she was overwhelmed by the awful truth.

'Sasha, you look exhausted. Why don't you turn in?' He stood up and came to her and reached down, taking her arm and helping her to her feet. He let her go immediately she was steady. 'I'm going for a walk before turning in,' he said softly, and then added with a smile, 'Don't wait up for me.'

She watched him walk away, down to the shoreline and veering off to the west. She pondered the fact that she had spent a good deal of time watching him, and apparently he had been watching her too, watching her fishing—but only to compare her with Henrietta. She had no one to compare him with—only his brother who wasn't worthy of comparison.

As she crawled under the mosquito net, in the shorts and thin cotton shirt that she had worn all day, and lay down on the bed of ferns that Richard had spread there she felt a numbing loneliness that she had never experienced before. She hoped it would lift because it wasn't pleasant and she didn't want to wake up in the morning feeling the same way. She wanted to feel different tomorrow. She vowed that she would try, but what form that feeling might take she didn't know.

CHAPTER SIX

SASHA turned and blinked open her eyes, wondering why she had been startled awake. The dawn was like a fire outside, muted by the mist of the mosquito net but nevertheless a flame of red and orange. A parakeet squawked close by and Sasha assumed that that was what had woken her.

She felt warmth on her shoulder and turned her head slightly. Richard lay beside her, on his side, his hand resting heavily on her shoulder as if to reassure her that he was there. As she moved her head her lips accidentally brushed his fingers and he stirred slightly but didn't move away from her.

She held her breath, eyes tightly closed, and felt a small rush of awareness chase down her spine. She opened her eyes and gazed at him in sleep, her stomach crawling with a sudden heat. She could smell his warmth and it was sensual. His thick dark lashes against the dark tan of his skin held her fascinated for a while. Her eyes lingered over every feature because he was asleep and she could do it without him knowing.

She drifted back to sleep and when she awoke later she was alone. She bathed in the sea after tying her hair up in a knot on the top of her head, and then dressed in clean shorts and vest-top. She was brushing out her gleaming hair when he returned with his video camera.

'What have you filmed?' she asked, throwing down her brush and kneeling over the fire to try and rouse the still hot embers.

'You swimming.'

She thought she might be blushing and concentrated on the fire while Richard filled a pan with bottled water to boil for coffee.

'Was it necessary?' she asked.

'Only for my personal records. This is a beautiful island,' he went on. 'I'd like to spend more time here but...'

'But what?' she prompted, sitting back on her haunches to look at him. She wasn't going to make a comment about his filming her for his personal records; that was best left alone.

'But I fear I might never want to leave.'

'Of course you will,' she told him sensibly. 'It won't be long before you start craving the luxuries of life.'

'And what are they?'

'All the things you've been used to in your privileged life—fast cars, wild women...'

He laughed. 'Is that the impression I give—fast cars and wild women?'

'Not here on the islands,' she admitted. She knew his life in New Zealand was a far cry from that here and yet he was relaxed—she could see it in the way he enjoyed himself. He was happy wandering the beach, he'd been moved by the dolphins, and he had appeared to enjoy cooking the supper last night over an open fire.

Geoff would have hated it all. Suddenly she wanted to know what Geoff had done with his life since she had left but, of course, she couldn't ask. Now she slightly regretted her decision to keep this trip with Richard on a business level. With caution she might have been able to find out what had become of his brother. When her father wrote he never mentioned him. All he was concerned with was trying to persuade her to come home.

'Have you family back in Auckland?' he suddenly asked, so unexpectedly that Sasha wondered if he had the ability to channel into her thoughts.

She rummaged in one of the packs for coffee. 'I thought we were supposed to be keeping this trip on a business level.'

'It's not easy,' he murmured, and took the coffee from her and tipped some into the pan of water on the fire.

No, it wasn't easy. She found herself wanting to know more about him, only because it was difficult to sustain conversation by merely talking about what they were going to eat and when.

'Yes, I have family back in Auckland,' she volunteered. If she was careful she needn't give too much away. 'But I haven't seen them for...since I came out here. I don't get on too well with my stepmother and my father is a busy man.'

'You can choose your friends but not your family,' he commented ruefully. 'What line of business is your father in?'

She didn't want to weave any more webs of lies around herself for fear of enmeshing herself in something she couldn't get out of. Skimming the truth wouldn't hurt, but anything deeper would, so to proceed with caution seemed the only choice.

'Banking,' she told him. 'This coffee's ready,' she said, diverting the conversation.

Richard took the pan from the fire and poured two cups, handing her one.

'Thompson, Thompson,' he mused. 'Can't say I've heard of him.'

Sasha nearly spilled the hot coffee down herself. She hoped he hadn't noticed. He knew her surname—her new surname. But there was nothing in that; John Harvey would have said it. She had been wise to change her name. Anyone who was anyone in Auckland would know the name McKenzie.

'There are a lot of bankers in Auckland,' she murmured.

'And I know most of them,' he muttered, and Sasha couldn't help her insides freezing. Too close—he was coming in too close. She prayed he wouldn't pursue this line of inquiry. She might make a mistake, slip up on her own banana skin of lies.

'My family is in banking too, though I try to steer clear of that side of the business,' he went on. 'I leave that to my younger brother, Geoff. He married into the Waite banking family last year—a second cousin of Henrietta's, actually. It's how I came to meet her and John Harvey.'

Sasha's head started spinning. Her hands shook as she lifted the plastic cup to her lips. The world was too small. She could feel it closing in on her, tightening around her heart till she could hardly breathe. So Geoff was married—no doubt a suitable marriage for the family— and to a relative of the awful Henrietta.

She didn't care that he was married, but it enhanced the pain she had suffered when she had discovered that he didn't love her and was only marrying her for a business merger. The drugs and the blonde were incidental, hurtful and worrying but only a part of the cause of her defection.

Sasha fought for control of her mouth. She must say something or he might get suspicious. But he didn't know who she really was and it was her fear of discovery that could be her undoing if she let it. And yet a small, intense part of her yearned to break out, to tell him all about herself so that he could form a true opinion of her, not one born of who she was supposed to be now.

'I get the impression you aren't too close to your family yourself,' she said at last.

'Do I give that impression?'

Oh, dear God, did he? Was she imagining all sorts of things in her panic to sound normal?

'You . . . you said, "you can choose your friends but not your family," and the way you said it . . .' She shrugged. 'Well, I just thought . . .'

'You're right—we're not particularly close. My brother always jumped when our father called; I simply looked the other way.'

'The black sheep of the family?'

'I suppose so, though it was never intentional. I just wanted to do things my way and with my father that was asking for trouble. And you—were you the rebel without a cause?'

Sasha shook her head and gazed out to sea, her eyes wide and clear. 'No, I was never a rebel. I tried to accept my stepmother but she didn't really accept me. The only time she took a real interest in me was when it looked like I was about to make a suitable marriage. When I backed out . . . when I decided it wasn't suitable at all . . . well, I was hardly flavour of the month.'

'And your father?'

She turned to him, her eyes narrowing. 'What about him?'

'How did he take it, your running away?'

Her pulses started to race uncertainly. He kept suggesting that she had run away; had she said she had? She couldn't remember but to make an issue of it would indicate that she had. She finished her coffee and threw the grounds into the fire where they hissed and exploded. 'I miss him,' she admitted. 'But he respects my independence.'

'I expect he misses you too.'

He said nothing more, just sat finishing his coffee and gazing out to sea as she had done. She followed his gaze and thought about her father, the ache for him deepened in that moment and she resented it because Richard had brought it about. She wished he hadn't come into her life because he made her think too deeply. He dragged her past up smack bang into the present, and it would affect her future if she wasn't careful.

But what of her future? How could she go back and face her father after the disgrace Geoff had brought on her with his wicked lies?

Though she loved her father a chasm had opened between them on his remarriage. She understood that he was torn between his love for Paula and his only daughter but she knew that to have protested her innocence would have been useless at the time. He would have sided with his wife and Paula would have done her best to blacken Sasha's name further. She had wanted the marriage into the Carlton family more than anyone, seeing the merger of the two families as another social step for her.

'We'd better get packed up,' she said at last, and in silence they did.

* * *

Sasha felt more relaxed once they reached the bigger island of Kailaghi. She was able to arrange accommodation for them close to the small clinic that served the island. It was a reed-roofed hut with the luxury of two separate rooms to sleep in. One of the doctors who toured the islands on his rounds had just left it vacant.

Sasha was amongst people she knew and spent the first day catching up on the local gossip, while Richard toured the island filming with a willing guide, one of the elders of the village who spoke English.

Sasha had laughed at the expression of amazement on Richard's face as she had introduced him to Ona. He was a formidable sight with his rough ebony skin and red hair, dressed in an indescribably filthy T-shirt and long, baggy shorts that a tourist had presented him with in gratitude for his island knowledge. Ona wore them proudly.

Sasha was still grinning when Richard returned as the sun was going down. He looked shattered and admitted that he was as he slumped in a rickety old cane chair on the shady veranda of the hut.

'I don't know whether to put you over my knee and slap you senseless for sending me off with Ona or...'

'Or what?' Sasha laughed. She handed him a glass of fresh lemon and lime juice and sat cross-legged on the wooden floor, watching him as he quenched his thirst.

His eyes were suddenly grave as he said, 'I was going to say "kiss you", but both would be a punishment to you, wouldn't they?'

Sasha said nothing. Feeling herself blushing again, she gulped at her juice.

'So you had a good time?' she said softly.

'It was an experience. He's a mine of useless information, very entertaining, and if I ever build a drive-in cinema on this island he'll be the manager. He's obsessed with videos and demanded I send him a copy of the film I took, him in prominence, of course.'

'Will you?' Sasha laughed.

'What, put in a drive-in—'

'No, send him the film.' She couldn't believe he was serious about the cinema.

'Does he have a player?'

Grinning, Sasha said, 'You won't believe this but the waiting room of the clinic doubles as the island's entertainment hut. They have a video player and see all the Western films they can get their hands on. Language is no barrier.'

'Unbelievable,' Richard breathed. 'And there was I promising faithfully to send him a copy for fear he might put a spell on me and I'd never walk again.'

'He might, so you'd better.'

'What's that round your neck?' he suddenly asked. 'Something to ward off evil spirits?' he added humorously.

Fingering the delicate necklace of pierced pink and white shells, she told him, 'It's *tafuliari*, once the currency, now simply to ward off other vendors. If you buy one and wear it the islanders will know you've made a contribution to the island's welfare and leave you alone. I wear it because I like it as well.'

He got up from the creaky old chair and came and squatted beside her. He reached out to examine the necklace and his fingers brushed her skin. His touch was like fiery-hot silk and she tensed against the prickly sensations that scoured her flesh.

'It's beautiful,' he breathed, and then his eyes came to hers. 'Like you, it's beautiful.'

There was no time to draw back from him and with a sudden realisation Sasha knew that she didn't want to. His mouth brushed sensuously against hers and then the sweet pressure deepened into a full-blown kiss that aroused every sense in her body. It lingered so long and so deeply that it spun her mind till she couldn't think straight. Bemused, she didn't protest; bemused, she knew she wanted it to go on and on; bemused, she realised she had missed his company today.

He drew back at last and looked at her, a long, lingering look that was as pleasurable as the kiss had been, and it was in that moment that Sasha knew they were both in trouble.

'I'm not going to apologise for that one,' he murmured roughly. 'It was needed and wanted by us both so don't spoil it by feigning hurt.' He took her chin gently and held her head steady in case she thought of running. His eyes darkened threateningly.

'In future, Sasha Thompson, don't palm me off with ravaged old natives to do the work I want you to do. I want you at my side morning, noon and night. You'd better get used to the idea because that's the way I want it.'

Slowly he got to his feet and stretched lazily, and it was as if he'd never spoken those last words. 'Any chance of a shower in this place or is it to be the ocean again?'

Wide-eyed and breathless, Sasha somehow got to her feet. She faced him, still bemused, still confused by her own see-sawing emotions. She should have been affronted by what he had done and said, and she wanted to be, but that kiss had swamped all the fight in her.

'There . . . there's a shower outside, behind the hut,' she found herself saying. 'It's . . . it's primitive—a bucket with a shower spray hanging from a tree . . .'

He needed no further bidding. He pushed aside the curtain which served as a door and returned with the towel she had laid out for him slung across his shoulder. He said nothing more as he went down the wooden steps and around to the back of the hut.

Slowly and nervously Sasha started to prepare a supper in the corner of the first room—the room she had taken for her own. His room was screened off by another curtain. She glanced at it with a trepidation she hadn't experienced when she had got the hut prepared for their stay.

Earlier she had been lulled into a sense of security by that curtain, thinking it far safer than sharing a reed shelter under the stars with him. 'Morning, noon and night,' he'd said. It wasn't difficult to know what he meant.

Her hands shook as she cut up the snake beans she'd bought at the market. She didn't want him, her sensibilities told her, and yet a battle warred inside her. She hardly knew him and yet he'd had a profound effect on her already and it was nothing, no, nothing to do with who he was. Did she want more from him? The question terrified her; the answer was elusive.

After supper, during which he told her all the tales Ona had regaled him with, he went for a stroll on his own across the clearing and down through the trees towards the beach. As Sasha cleared away she wondered what he thought about on these nocturnal walks of his. Was he fighting his conscience? He'd made it plain that he wanted her, but Henrietta . . .

She didn't want to think about her so didn't.

Later, when he still hadn't returned, she crawled into bed under her mosquito net and lay facing the timber wall, hoping he would think her asleep, nervous in case he didn't.

He was making breakfast the next morning when she awoke. The trouble was that the kitchen area was in another corner of the room she was lying in. She lifted the net and peered out. He had his back to her and was stirring a pan of coffee over the single gas ring.

'I'd like to get up if you don't mind.'

'There's nothing to stop you,' he said without turning.

'I . . . I haven't got any clothes on.'

'Grow up, Sasha. I haven't got eyes in the back of my head,' he snapped.

'OK, moody!'

Sasha pushed aside the net, swung her legs to the floor, draped the single sheet around her, grabbed her clothes from a chair and hurried into his room to dress.

He was out on the veranda when she emerged. She joined him, clothed, but her hair still tousled by a restless night.

'So you had as rough a night as I did?' he commented, his eyes glancing at the tumble of hair around her shoulders.

Sasha pushed it back self-consciously. 'The heat in that hut is unbearable.'

'We were better off under the stars.'

'Maybe,' she murmured, sipping her coffee. 'Is that why you're so grumpy this morning—a bad night?' She looked at him cautiously. Was he in a mood that might drag through the day?

'I wasn't grumpy when I got up; I got that way when a certain person came over all coy about getting out of bed.'

'I told you, I didn't have any clothes on!' Sasha protested.

'Did it matter?'

She wondered if he was teasing her. 'Yes, it did matter. I'd be asking for trouble flashing around naked, wouldn't I?'

'The trouble you want and the trouble I can give you,' he said, and there was a definite gleam of humour in his eyes.

Sasha was not placated by it. 'And what you are hinting at *would* be trouble, Richard. Trouble for you and Henrietta and trouble for me because... because—'

'Because what—you want to be a nun?'

'Would it make any difference to you if I *did* want to be a nun?'

'An enormous difference,' he grated. 'I'd have to step up the pressure to save you from an ill-suited vocation for a woman with your looks, your body and the needs you are doing your best to bury under an avalanche of emotional baggage.'

'Is all this because I was in *my* bed last night instead of yours when you came back?' she drawled knowingly.

He put his cup down on the table in front of him and leaned across the table towards her. 'I wanted you last night, and if I was anyone but old-fashioned Richard Carlton it wouldn't have mattered whose bed you were in. My problem is that I'm far too open about my needs, whereas you try to wrap yours in a cloak of prudery.'

Sasha smiled thinly. 'My, what a load of tired old clichés—"an avalanche of emotional baggage",' she mimicked. '"A cloak of prudery".' She leaned towards him and their noses nearly touched. 'You know what you sound like? A male chauvinist pig who thinks that women who say no really mean yes.'

She went to get up but suddenly his hand caught her wrist and swung her round to his side of the table. The intention was to pull her down onto his lap but something went horribly wrong. The rickety old chair gave under them both, sprawling them on the deck of the veranda. With astonishing speed and dexterity he somehow manipulated her under him and held her arms above her head.

'Regrettably I'm crazy about you,' he grated, his mouth only centimetres from hers.

Sasha wriggled helplessly under him. 'You're just crazy!' she panted.

'That as well,' he agreed. 'Now you just hold still while I kiss you and prove that when *you* say no you mean yes!'

'Oh, yeah? Just you try...just you try, you...you chauvinist pig!'

'Clichés, clichés,' he teased, and then there were no centimetres between their lips, nothing but hot, sweet moisture and a pressure so demanding, so sure that she would succumb to it that it was inevitable she would. The length of his body pressed dangerously against the heat of her own, so erotically that her spine arched in defence against the onslaught of such blatant need.

As his lips crushed hers, devouring and insatiable, his taut body aroused every inch of hers till there was fire on her skin at every pulse-point. She burned in his arms;

her head spun as he drew away from her lips and ran his tongue down the column of her throat, leaving her mouth free to protest what he had claimed she didn't mean.

But there were no protests, not from her lips or her senses, because what he was doing was such ecstasy. His mouth was a balm on her fiery skin, a soothing balm of sensuality, playing down her throat, across her shoulder as he eased aside her flimsy cotton shirt.

As his fingers brushed her skin she realised that her hands were free but they might as well have been in chains for the use they were to her. They lay above her head where he had left them, fists clenched tightly—as tightly as her heart within her. She lay helpless beneath him, knowing she shouldn't, knowing she was giving him fuel for his actions, knowing he was so damned right.

Her shirt came apart at her breasts and her heart came alive as his hand brushed her nipple softly, testing and then caressing so tenderly—small circular movements that teased and tantalised and had her blood surging through her like a torrent of fluid fire. Please, no. Please, yes. The words were there in her throat, trapped by a swelling of need so strong that it overwhelmed all other emotions.

His mouth, closing over her inflamed peak, and urgent now as his arousal reached danger point, forced a heated gasp of shock from her throat—a gasp that shuddered through her, a gasp that seemed to power him on. She could feel his arousal hard against her groin and then suddenly her arms moved involuntarily and they were on his shoulders, her fingers pressing desperately into his shirt, wanting to push him away yet not.

The pressure on her breasts eased, then came back again, his tongue teasing, and then his lips were there again, hot and demanding. The tears came then and she didn't know why. Her hands on his shoulders relaxed and a great weakness enfolded her and a sob caught in her throat. His mouth came to hers then—a mouth so comforting that she knew the pressure was off. A tender, tender kiss grazed her lips and then he was kissing the tears from her face.

'Too soon,' he grated at last, and drew back from her.

She opened her tear-filled eyes and looked up at him, not knowing why her emotions had spilled over so weakly. He eased away from her and gently pulled her up into a sitting position. He held her by one shoulder and his other hand came to her face, and with the backs of his fingers he brushed the tears from her cheeks.

'I could kill him for this,' he said roughly.

'K-kill who?' she croaked in a whisper.

'That hell of a bastard.'

Sasha lowered her head, shaking it, spilling more tears from her eyes. 'It isn't that, not him,' she uttered weakly.

He lifted her chin and his eyes were smoky with concern as he looked at her. 'What is it, then? Is it me?'

How could she tell him that it was? She wanted him; what had just happened had proved to her what she hadn't been able to admit from the start. She had suppressed her attraction to him from the very beginning, unconsciously at first, not even knowing that what powered her reticence was in fact that damned attraction to him.

What wicked games the heart and the reluctant mind could play. How devious were the workings of the subconscious. And she had fought him because he was who he was—the brother of the man she had run from. If she fell in love with him, which she now thought was a miserable possibility, what then?

'Sasha, tell me what you're thinking,' he pleaded.

She shook her head again. 'I don't know what I'm thinking,' she admitted emotionally. 'I know what happened just now was what you wanted to happen. You wanted to prove a point and—'

'It was more than that. I wanted to make love to you but I can't do it on my own. I want you to want it too. I thought you did, and then the stand-off and the tears.'

'I...I'm sorry. I'm not a tease but—'

'You're afraid?' She didn't answer, just lowered her lashes again. 'I wouldn't hurt you,' he went on. 'I'm not the lover that messed you up.'

She raised her lashes and looked at him, feeling stronger now, her emotions levelling. She sensed that he wouldn't hurt her, not intentionally, but maybe he wouldn't be able to help it. She wanted to trust him and very nearly did, but he was a Carlton and the other one in her life had been such a rat. She was torn, so terribly torn between wanting him and rejecting him to save the hurt.

She swallowed and spoke. 'You are the first man that has touched me since...since—'

'Since your lover?'

Sasha tried to smile; she sniffed at the same time. 'My lover was never my lover,' she admitted, 'if you know what I mean.'

His eyes darkened as if he didn't believe her and Sasha's heart slumped. Who would believe that in this day and age a couple could be engaged to be married and not consummate the union before the wedding day? He obviously wouldn't.

She drew a breath before going on. 'When I said touch I meant just that: touch.' Her eyes were suddenly misty again. 'You touched me; you caressed me; the tears came because...because it...it revealed how empty my life has been. But really I'm glad the tears came because if they hadn't I might have done...might have let you make love to me.'

'And really you didn't want to.' He said it but didn't sound convinced.

'I did want it,' she admitted, surprised by her own honesty, but realising that if she tried to explain truthfully he might ease the pressure from her. 'But wanting and taking aren't always wise.

'I'm not a prude. I'm not nursing a broken heart over another man. I want what you want. There, I've admitted it. I want sex, if you like. Sex is what it's all about but I don't know how I'd feel after, or even during it. I don't know if you can fill my loneliness. You don't have any empty pockets in your life to fill. I do.'

He let out a ragged sigh as if he was disappointed in her. 'You have some problems, do you know that?'

She shook her head. 'I don't have any problems, but you're putting pressure on me that could give me problems.'

'What are you afraid of?'

How could she tell him she was afraid that if they got in too deep she would have to run again? If they did have an affair, if that affair developed into love, what then?

She couldn't fit into his life; that would be impossible. To fit into his future he'd have to know her past. She had been about to marry his brother—the brother who had blackened her name so disgustingly that a relationship with another Carlton would be ... impossible.

'I'm afraid of you, if you must know,' she told him softly. She got up, smoothed her hands down her shorts and looked down at him. 'I know so little about you.' It was a poor response but all she could offer.

He got to his feet and faced her. 'There's one way of finding out more,' he suggested quietly.

She afforded him a grim smile, knowing what he meant. 'That's hardly the answer. Just because two people make love it doesn't mean they get to know each other better.'

'I didn't say that.'

'You meant it, though. Sex only breaks down the inhibitions of the body—'

'And you want the inhibitions of your mind sorted out?'

Sasha rubbed her forehead. She didn't know; all she knew was that an intimacy with this man, though undoubtedly pleasurable, would be a bad mistake.

'I'm not a psychiatrist,' he told her after a long pause. He lifted her chin and looked deep into her green eyes. 'As well as wanting to get into your body I also want to get into your psyche, but I might not find that as agreeable as the physical possession. Is that what you are afraid of—me finding something to my distaste?'

In shocked horror she widened her eyes. It was as if he knew—as if he knew everything about her and Geoff. But how many times had she thought that only to have convinced herself that he couldn't possibly know? If he did, this was a punishment. The ultimate revenge—to make her love him so that he could reject her as she had rejected his brother. Oh, why wouldn't her mind just close down? She didn't want to think of such possibilities.

She couldn't bear him looking at her so quizzically. She went to turn away but he wouldn't let her. He held her by her shoulders.

'You and I are in for a tough time, Sasha, because we want each other. Now, I could kick around for weeks waiting for you to drop that false purity of yours and allow me into your bed and into your heart, but it would be hard going and I'm all for an easy life. So I'm going to try and make life simple for us both, the only way I can.' His eyes darkened determinedly.

'I want you in my bed tonight. Not here—the conditions aren't right. We're moving on to somewhere more intimate, to somewhere where the earth is going to move for us under the stars. I'm going to make love to you so long and intensely that "inhibitions" is a word you'll soon forget.'

His hand reached up and slid beneath her limp shirt, and very slowly he brushed the back of his hand across her breasts. Her reaction was instantaneous and an involuntary give-away of how deeply his proposal had got to her. Her breasts swelled under the sensuous touch; her nipples peaked and throbbed with desire.

To protest would have been a waste of precious breath as the heat of the island, the heat of him pressed down and around her. No escape and did she want it? She didn't know; all she knew was that his touch was temptation, his words a sexual spur to her senses.

As his hand dropped away and he smiled benignly she knew that she couldn't rouse a protest to her lips. She was torn inside—torn by her needs and torn by the eventual outcome of those needs—because once he possessed her she would lose control. And then what? She didn't know.

CHAPTER SEVEN

'So, HERE we are—Infidelity Island,' Sasha quipped sarcastically as they beached the canoes once again. They had chugged around several islands looking for a suitable spot to land and Richard had decided on this one. In the time it had taken for him to make up his mind her fighting form had come back.

He had intimidated her back on Kailaghi—so much so that they had packed up and left with her scarcely uttering a word. Now she'd had time to collect her wits and they were raring to go.

'That has a harmonious ring to it,' he said equally sarcastically as he flopped down on the sand to catch his breath after the exertion of hauling the canoes in. 'Not very apt, though. You're not married and nor am I. Infidelity doesn't come into it.'

Sasha threw herself down yards away from him, cupped her hands behind her head and closed her eyes against the glare of the sun. 'Yes, well, the Isle of Lust is more like it, I suppose.'

She heard him laugh and came up on her elbows to look across at him.

'This is all a game to you, isn't it?'

He sat up and clutched his knees. He didn't look at her, just tossed tiny pink shells into the surf foaming on the shore.

'No, it isn't a game, sweetheart. I'm taking it all quite seriously; you're the one seeing it as lusterama in Technicolor.'

'So what is "it"? Love, I suppose. Love spelt lust. What do you know about love?'

'About as much as you do, which is a minimal amount, I guess.'

Sasha stared sullenly out to sea, her heart thumping miserably. Why had she brought the word love into it? He hadn't. What did she know about love? She'd never been there; apparently nor had he. What a couple of cynics they were.

'Aren't you in love with Henrietta?' she asked quietly.

'Is that what's still bothering you? Is that what put infidelity in your mind?'

He was looking at her now; she felt his eyes on her—she always could. Even with her back to him she knew when he was looking at her. She sat up properly and gathered her arms around her knees as he had.

'She's in your life,' she muttered.

'But not in my bed or my heart, I told you that.'

'Not properly you didn't. I saw the way she was throwing poisoned darts at you at her uncle's party, angry with you and hating me because you were determined to spend time with me—her time.'

'She's a possessive lady.'

'She's a lady in love,' Sasha bit out.

'Not with me. She might think she is but she isn't because she's not open to love. She's very much open to nailing herself a good marriage, though. As one of Auckland society yourself you'll know the truth of that.'

Her stomach tightened as it always did when he came up with something so close to her past. 'I didn't say I was from Auckland society,' she protested, nerves on alert again. She knew she hadn't, was positive of it.

'I put two and two together,' he said quickly, and then suddenly got to his feet. 'Come on, we've got work to do.'

Sasha shot to her feet, brushing the sand from the seat of her shorts, glad that he was so dismissive suddenly. 'Yes, of course. We have to get the nuptial hut up before—'

'My God, where's the romance in your soul?' he growled but he was really teasing.

Sasha fought for her humour but couldn't raise much more than a slice of biting sarcasm. 'Romance? Romance is a seven-letter dirty word if you ask me!'

'I see I'm going to have to work on that,' he threatened, and started to unload the canoes.

'You won't have time,' she told him. 'You have a house to build, some scavenging for fresh fruit to do, and a fire to prepare before nightfall. *I'm* going fishing.'

She helped him unload the second canoe and then sprang into it and paddled out to sea, leaving him watching her thoughtfully as she drew further away from him.

She wondered if he really did know her true identity, and, if he didn't, whether she should tell him. She wondered what difference it would make if he did know the truth. Would he believe all those lies? Would he hate her for it? How impossible it all was. They might have an affair—Richard seemed convinced that they would— but it could *only* be an affair because there was no hope for a future for them, not as a couple.

She was going too fast, she reprimanded herself. Nothing had happened yet; words had been bandied, lips had touched, hearts—well, hers at least—had fluttered, that was all. Nothing life-threatening.

Later she returned with her catch—a good haul considering she'd had to abort the trip so soon. A school of inquisitive dolphins had approached and made further fishing impossible. She hadn't joined them for some frolicking because she hadn't wanted to, not alone without Richard.

As she'd paddled her way back to shore she'd acknowledged the feeling inside her—this feeling of wanting to be a pair with Richard. It was why she had taken him out that first time—to share it with him.

She beached the canoe, took the net of fish out of the bottom of the boat and her eyes searched the beach for him. Was this funny feeling inside her blossoming into love?

As she wandered up the beach and through the jungle to look for the man who had troubled her so, she thought that a bit of honesty to herself, for herself, was ready to be born.

She did want love; more than anything else in the world she wanted someone to love and to give her the love that had eluded her so far in her life. But it was a new realisation to her—one that had only come about since Richard had come into her life. It needed to be treated with caution.

Could she love Richard? Her heart squeezed at the thought of him, and it had done from the moment she had first met him on Ko-chi's boat. Was that enough to agree to what he wanted—her in his bed? If she allowed it, would she know for sure how she felt? But *allowing* it wasn't the right approach. She should want it badly enough for it to dispel her past, to fill her present with sunshine and light and to give her future the joy of hope.

'Oh, dear God!' she breathed in wonderment as she stepped into a small clearing. Her heart squeezed so tightly at the sight before her eyes that she felt faint with the pressure. She knew then, in that blinding moment as her eyes feasted on the spellbinding beauty of what he'd done, that love for this man was a strong possibility. How could she fail to be tempted?

They had thought the island was uninhabited and it was now, but once a small community had lived here. There was a group of abandoned thatched huts on stilts, gathered in a half-circle, ravaged by seasons of rain and storms, some with their primitive roofs torn open to the skies. But one stood resolutely out from the others, intact and ... and bedecked with tropical flowers.

Biting her lip, her eyes wide with surprise, she hesitantly stepped further into the clearing. The open doorway of the raised hut was festooned with hibiscus, bougainvillea and orchids woven into the supports to create a floral archway.

There was a small veranda with a rickety wooden rail and it was plaited with a flowery creeper, the deck carpeted with palm leaves and ferns. The pathway to the hut was a carpet of ferns liberally sprinkled with flower petals.

Stunned by the sight of the luscious hut set in the parched clearing, she just stood and stared for a few minutes, and then slowly she took the petal-strewn path to the steps that led up to it.

'Richard!' she called lightly once she was on the veranda. There was no sign of him. Across the top of the doorway was a strip of bark and scratched on it were three words: 'THE LOVE HUT'. She was about to enter the dark, secret place when she heard a sound behind her and swung round.

He stood a few feet from the hut, his arms full of driftwood for a fire.

'Enter those who dare,' Richard said softly, his mouth curved into a tempting smile.

'You rat,' she breathed under her breath so that he couldn't hear. 'You...you did all this?' she whispered for his ears.

'Who else?' he said, and let the driftwood drop at the bottom of the steps. He came up and stood beside her and took her hand in his. His touch was warm and tempting and she didn't pull away. 'Aren't you impressed?'

She nodded. 'Yes, very, but...' It hurt too. So determined to bed her, he had gone to these extraordinary lengths to impress her. She really wasn't sure of the depth of his sincerity.

He raised a brow, waiting for her to say something more, not helping her by waiting.

'It...it's a surprise,' she murmured. 'I didn't expect...' Her voice trailed to nothing. She honestly didn't know what else to say. The significance of it all was obvious to her but still she was lost for words.

'If you enter the commitment is made, Sasha,' he whispered, and he let go of her hand and stepped out of her way as if he was giving her the freedom to make the choice.

It was the Garden of Eden, temptation. One step and the commitment would be made. But what commitment? He saw all this as something for the moment, and she would have to see it that way too because there was no way forward for them, no future in anything they might do together. In that moment Sasha felt a despair that crushed the temptation.

She turned, her eyes misty, and brushed past him, down the steps and across the clearing, and she didn't stop running till she was on the hot white beach. Only then did she slow her pace because the heat and the humidity were sapping her strength.

She walked along the shore to the far end of the island where a crop of palm trees offered shelter. She sank beneath them and with both hands held the place where her heart pounded. It hurt so much and the thoughts that pounded in her head hurt too.

She was sick of blindly wandering around in a wilderness of loneliness. She wanted to belong. She wanted to belong to Richard. She couldn't believe that she was thinking this way, even considering giving herself to the brother of the man who had betrayed her so. But he was different, she reminded herself—so very different from any man she had met.

She awoke hours later, hot and aching, the pressure inside her temples so intense that she wanted to cry with the pain of it. She sat up and grasped her knees tightly and stared out to a crimson sunset that was almost blinding in a last fiery burst of aggression before it died.

'There's a message there,' she mused quietly, her voice the only sound. 'The sun comes up and the sun goes down and nothing in the world can change it.'

And she couldn't change this feeling inside her—this feeling of wanting to be wanted, this feeling of wanting to give too. So what had the wretched sun to do with it and what was the message she was seeking? That life was transient? she wondered as she got up, dusted herself down and headed back to the clearing and Richard. Well, tomorrow the sun would come up whatever she decided; that was the only certainty.

Richard was baking the fish in the ashes of the fire when she got back. The fire was the only light, casting a shimmer of illumination onto the Love Hut behind him. She could just see that he'd laid a cloth on the veranda for them to eat from. No tables or chairs, just the ferns and the flowers and the sweet scents of a tropical night.

'Do you feel better?' he murmured as she squatted in the dirt next to him and he prodded the fish with a stick.

'A little,' she said softly.

He said nothing for a while—a while in which Sasha evaluated the whole scene around her. Two people sitting in the dust, cooking food on an open fire, the beautiful, flower-swathed hut behind them, just waiting, no one to touch them in this secret world of theirs.

'I've put too much pressure on you,' he said at last. His voice was clipped and decisive. 'I won't any more. We'll sleep in that hut together because we have no choice; it's all there is. But no more pressure. I don't want to hurt you.'

She nodded and understood and in a way she loved him for that.

They ate their meal in silence and then Richard got up and he didn't have to say it was time for his nocturnal wanderings. He just wandered off and Sasha watched him as she had done before, wondering what he was thinking and hoping she was a part of it.

She lifted the candles they always had to hand and lit one, and, holding it carefully, her feet cushioned by ferns, she gazed into the hut from the doorway. It was as beautiful inside as out. There was just the one room. Creepers were strung along the walls of the hut, flowers too. The floor was thick with a mattress of cushiony ferns.

Suddenly the candle flickered in her hand and the barometer of her spine tingled out a warning; it heralded a fear that was nothing to do with temptation. She listened to the silence. There wasn't a sound...no cicadas and crickets, no nocturnal squawk of wildlife, nothing but that strange silence...and she knew and cursed herself out loud for not knowing sooner.

She blew out the candle, stepped outside and looked across at the palms, so incredibly tall and just silhouetted against the night sky. The tips of the palm-fronds wavered dangerously; soon the skirts would be up and... Sasha started to run for Richard; as she ran she heard the low, ominous moan in the distance and the first splashes of rain started to fall.

'Richard!' she screamed, crashing through the vegetation on the edge of the beach. 'Richard!'

It was so dark that she could hardly see. She reached the beach and could just see him standing at the water's edge. The wind had erupted but he didn't seem aware of it as it billowed his shirt.

'Richard!' she cried again, and this time he heard and turned to her. 'There's a storm coming, a squall; come quickly. No, wait—the canoes. We'll have to drag them further up.' Oh, God, she couldn't think straight. 'Ropes—we'll need ropes to lash down the roof of the hut.'

'They're there,' he responded quickly. 'I took everything up to the clearing.'

They both ran to the canoes and hauled them further up the beach. 'I should have known,' she wailed as they sped through the undergrowth to the clearing, wishing she'd paid more attention to the sky at sunset instead of dreaming. 'We'll have to work quickly—'

'I'll see to it,' he ordered. 'You get what you can under cover.'

First Sasha kicked out the dying embers of the fire in case the rain didn't douse it and sparks flared up and ignited the hut. She lit a battery-operated lamp and hung it on the veranda so that she could see to work.

She hauled everything she thought they might need into the one room of the hut, brought the lamp in to light the room and then tore back outside to help Richard.

'Get back inside,' he yelled from the roof where he was straddled across the palm-fronds, lashing them down with ropes. Already the rain was coming down at full pelt. They were both soaked through to the skin.

'I can help,' she cried, and climbed up the veranda to reach the roof.

Without further argument he threw her the end of the rope. She pulled it taut, looped it across a wooden bracket and tied it fast. The rope stung her fingers but she didn't fuss. They had to make the hut secure; it was imperative.

'The window and the door,' Richard called across the roof, and they both scrambled down onto the veranda. Sasha stood bemused, not knowing how they could block the open doorway. When the full force of the storm hit them the wind would tear into the opening and pluck the hut up as if it were a paper bag.

Suddenly Richard was running across the clearing to the huts that had been ravaged by previous storms. He started ripping at the side of one which was still intact but for the roof, and Sasha ran out to help him.

'Go back to the hut, Sasha,' he ordered heatedly. 'It isn't safe out here.' As if to prove him right a great gust of furious wind hit her, catching her unawares, and she hurtled up against the side of the hut and it gave under her weight.

'Well, that's one way of doing it,' she cried as she scrambled to her feet, Richard stooping to help her.

'Now will you do as you're told?' he growled threateningly, grasping her so tightly that he hurt her.

'No, I won't!' she flashed back. 'It will be easier and quicker with two. Don't waste time arguing.'

Together they dragged as much of the wattled cane as they could manage across the clearing. With the machete Richard hacked a piece to the shape of the door while Sasha secured the flap down over the gaping window from the inside. Then she turned to help with the door, holding it in place for him as he secured it tightly with the rest of the rope.

At last it was done and, breathless and with perspiration and rain coursing from their faces, they stared at each other. Richard grinned.

'You're some girl Friday, you know.'

Sasha gave him a weak smile. 'And for a sophisticate you haven't done badly yourself.'

'I know it must sound out of place but I enjoyed it— battling with the elements, you and me against the world.'

Raking a hand through her wet hair, Sasha smiled again. 'You get your kicks out of some odd situations.'

'I didn't before I met you.'

He held her eyes momentarily and Sasha was the first to break the contact. She shivered slightly although the hut was hot and stuffy. The wind and rain raged outside but they were well protected inside.

She picked at her sopping wet shirt. 'We'd better get into dry clothes. I've put yours out over there.' She nodded in the direction of the clean shirt and shorts she'd laid over his camera equipment in the corner of the room and was relieved when he went straight to them without making any suggestive comments about them undressing in front of each other.

Sasha turned her back on him, scooped her wet shirt over her head and, without looking at him, proceeded to pull on a clean T-shirt, wishing she'd had the nerve to towel herself dry first. The T-shirt covered her body so she felt no embarrassment at kicking off her wet shorts. She hurried into clean ones and only then relaxed. When she turned back to him he was dressed and squatting down by the radio they always carried.

'You won't get anything,' she told him, 'not till the wind dies down.'

'I thought I might pick up some weather warnings.'

'Too late. If it's any consolation I don't think this will be a big one. They would have warned us on Kailaghi if it was going to be a wicked one. We're probably getting the tail-end of a cyclone that is raging elsewhere, or perhaps just a South Pacific squall.'

As if to dispute her theory there was a sudden roar of wind which shook the whole hut and made Sasha give an involuntary cry of fright. She was in his arms before she could stop herself. She suddenly realised that she was very frightened. The roar of the wind went on and on, blasting at the hut, thankfully in vain.

He held her tightly against him and she could hear the steady beat of his heart against her chest. He wasn't afraid and she drew great comfort from him, solid and reliable against her. She trusted him, she wanted to be with him, and in her heart she knew she wanted to be with him for ever.

She pulled back when the roar softened to a dull thud of impatience as the wind prodded threateningly at the small island. The Love Hut was holding up and was their sanctuary for however long it would take for the storm to wear itself out.

'I'm sorry,' she uttered helplessly as he held her shoulders comfortingly.

'Don't apologise for being afraid.'

'I'm not... not really afraid. It's just that I've always been at the bungalow in Suya or at the hospital complex during these storms. They were built to stand up to the forces.'

'And whoever lived here on this island before built these huts in the most protected place. We'll be safe, don't worry.'

She smiled ruefully up at him. 'This hut was the only one left standing.'

He smiled. 'Because it's special, I guess.' He lifted her chin and planted a very small kiss of reassurance on her lips. 'Now I'm going to brew up some coffee and I think we ought to get some rest. With any luck we should sleep the storm out.'

He let her go and Sasha felt the loss of his strong arms about her. She felt another loss too, and it felt suspiciously like a rejection. He wanted to *sleep* the storm out.

Her hands trembled slightly as she went for the blankets and laid them out at the other end of the hut. She heard the gentle hiss of the portable gas ring as he lit it carefully, and though it was only a gentle hiss it penetrated deep into her soul.

She had expected him to make the suggestion that they *love* the storm out. How would she be able to sleep feeling the way she did—rejected? But how contrary of her to feel that rejection. She had fought him long enough and now...and now that she didn't want to fight him any more all he wanted to do was sleep.

'Will we need all those blankets?' he asked while brewing the coffee. 'It's like an oven in here.'

Sasha sat cross-legged on a blanket and examined her hands. They were red and stinging from the friction of the rope. 'It's warm now but the rain and wind will soon lower the temperature. We'll probably be shivering in the middle of the night.'

'What have you done?'

'Nothing.' She slid her hands under her, not wanting to show her vulnerability.

He came to her. 'Let me see.' He took her hands in his and turned the palms up and she saw him wince. He raised them to his lips and kissed them gently and Sasha closed her eyes and bit her lip.

'First-aid kit?' he murmured, and she opened her eyes and nodded towards the other side of the hut.

'Don't go away,' he joked, and went for the box.

He squatted down beside her, bathed her burning palms and fingers with a cooling lotion and then dabbed cream gently over the friction marks. Then he raised her chin to look into her face and kissed the tears from her cheeks. She hadn't even realised that she was crying.

'Do they hurt that much?' he breathed with concern.

She shook her head. 'No...it's just...'

'You're afraid?' he prompted quietly.

She tried to smile. 'A bit. I don't know what I'd have done if I'd been alone on this island.'

'You wouldn't be on this island if it wasn't for me,' he reasoned. His eyes darkened. 'I shouldn't have insisted on bringing you here. It was totally irresponsible on my part.' His eyes glimmered in the light above their heads. 'I'll never forgive myself if anything happens to you.'

He said it with such passion that it set Sasha's heart racing. He cared; he really cared. She felt tears brimming again, and to divert him she reminded him of the coffee bubbling on the ring.

He poured two cups, sweetened them heavily and brought them back to her.

'Drink this and try and get some rest, Sasha. I'm here, you're safe and I promise you you always will be.'

Sleepily she took the coffee from him and sipped it gratefully. She was suddenly so exhausted that she couldn't begin to analyse what he meant about keeping her safe for always. All she could think was that at the moment she did feel safe with him. And it was a good feeling, like the feeling she'd had in the wreck of the plane back at Suya—that something good had come out of a potentially dangerous situation.

She finished her coffee and curled up on the blanket, and as her eyelids fluttered she felt Richard cover her with another blanket and his lips brush her brow. Then a delicious drowsiness overcame her.

She awoke later and the hut was in darkness. The wind was still howling and the rain lashed the roof but the hut was solid and secure around them. And Richard was solid and secure next to her and she drew great comfort from him. She stirred and turned to him and it was as if that was what he had been waiting for. His arms came around her and his lips sought hers. The time had come as she'd known it had to, and she welcomed it.

Neither spoke a word because it wasn't needed. Sasha knew how she felt—a deep feeling for this man who had come into her life so unexpectedly—and she sensed that his feelings were deep too because his kisses were so intense. His arms enfolded her and held her so close and tenderly that the gesture couldn't have been inspired by anything else but true feeling.

There was no thought of the future or the past. Sasha lost herself in a sweet rapture she'd never felt before. She ached for him but there was no hurry on his part. He was a sensual lover, his caresses so sure and confident, and she thrilled to every one.

He gave her confidence and she wasn't afraid to love him. She touched him, smoothing her hands across his broad shoulders, and felt the tightening of his muscles beneath her fingers. Her love for him pulsed deep inside her, a new awakening as he mouthed kisses across her throat and his hands lifted her T-shirt to touch the silken flesh beneath. Her breasts responded with the same intensity of feeling and she moaned softly—a small sound that couldn't be heard above the moan of the wind and rain.

Her breasts, her stomach, her inner thighs all responded to his magical touch. It was fire on her skin, heightening her desire till her breathing quickened. She fumbled with his clothes, wanting to touch and feel his nakedness against her, wanting to feel the pressure of his need hard against her.

Then they were free and she was so drugged by her senses that she was hardly aware that he had eased their clothes away from their heated bodies. The feel of him was ecstasy, so strong and warm and urgent, and there was nothing that could have stopped her in that moment of giving.

She stirred under him as he covered her body with his, kissing her lips and drawing her breath from her very soul. He cupped her bottom and lifted her hard against him, and his arousal was pure joy and she wanted him, now and for ever.

His fingers on her inner thigh were so exquisitely erotic—small caresses of teasing fire that blazed her senses till she wanted to cry out her need so that he wouldn't delay any longer.

She heard his soft moan of pleasure in her hair as his fingers sought her secret self. The rhythm of the movement was almost too much to bear and she writhed against him, quietly sobbing out her need as the wind and rain raged all around them. And when she thought she could bear no more of his sensuous torture he moved across her and his penetration was so deep and powerful that she bit hard on her lower lip, arching her back in a small convulsion of joy and pain.

He stilled for a second and she felt the gasp of his breath on her face, and she was suddenly afraid that he would pull back from her so she clung to him, pressing her warm mouth to his throat till he responded with the desire and need that neither could hold back from.

Deep thrusts of passion drove them on till Sasha thought she would die with the intensity of feeling that

was taking her to a place she had never been to before—
a place where heat and liquid fire blazed within her,
swelled and blossomed.

Then a miracle happened as he moved his hand down
and caressed a part of her that exploded her passion.
She climaxed, crying out her pleasure, and he was moving
inside her again, enhancing the sweet agony, drawing it
onwards and outwards like a fiery balloon of liquid
pleasure.

He swelled and instinctively she knew, and she drew
him harder into her, wanting to give him everything of
her—her body, her heart, her very soul. He shuddered
into her, his fingers biting into the soft flesh of her hips,
grasping her as the release powered through him, leaving
his whole body burning and shaking with sensation.

They lay together on their mattress of forest ferns,
bodies cooling, hearts softening, eyelids drooping. Sasha
had never known such complete and utter happiness,
never known such intensity of strength as they had
powered into their lovemaking.

She felt him move his arm around her to draw her
head down to his shoulder. His mouth brushed across
her forehead and she let out a small sigh of utter con-
tentment as she silently mouthed her love for him against
his fragrant skin.

He wasn't aware of it because he was already asleep,
and she didn't mind because he must surely know she
loved him anyway. He must know that she had given
more than her body this stormy night. So much more.

CHAPTER EIGHT

SASHA fumbled with the rope at the door of the hut, trying not to wake Richard. She eased the door inwards, taking furtive glances over her shoulder at him, holding the door steady to minimise the creaking of the brittle cane.

She took a deep breath of humid hot air as she stood on the veranda. The rain had stopped but she smelt more on the air and the thick belt of cloud over the island confirmed it. The wind had dropped dramatically, though.

She ran through the jungle to the beach, naked but for a sarong tied around her waist. She had never felt such freedom of spirit. It was like a rebirth—the first day of the rest of her life.

Stripping off the sarong, she cast it aside and the crimson silk floated down to the sand as she plunged into the sea, her arms upraised and her head tilted up to summon the sun to her flushed face. It obliged her momentarily, and it was enough to make her heart surge with happiness.

She *was* happy, for the first time in so long. And she was going to stay happy, for as long as... She didn't know for how long but she did know that she wasn't going to think negatively. *This* was the time—no other—and she was going to live it.

'Sasha! Sasha! What the devil do you think you're doing?'

She heard the roar of his voice and stilled herself in the water, staring at him, stunned by his furious tone. She swam towards him, feeling the euphoria seeping from her limbs.

He was waiting for her on the edge of the surf, already dressed in shorts and T-shirt, her sarong dangling from one hand. She was suddenly hit with embarrassment at her naked state. After the passion of the night she shouldn't have felt that way but he was dressed and she wasn't.

'Are you crazy?' He flung the crimson silk around her shoulders, tightening it around her to cover her nakedness. 'You could have drowned out there. The sea is like a tempest—'

'It isn't,' she insisted, wriggling to get her arms free. 'I can read the sea—'

'You can't read the undercurrents after a storm like last night's,' he thrust back at her fiercely, his eyes dark with anger.

Sasha didn't argue that one of the island elders had taught her how to read the sea and the currents and that she had known she was perfectly safe out there. She didn't argue because she understood his anger and her heart warmed to it. She lifted her hands to the sides of his face and smiled up at him.

'I was all right, Richard,' she reassured him softly. 'I really was.'

She could feel the tension in his facial muscles; her hands dropped to his upper arms and she felt steel-hard muscle under her fingertips. Slowly she let her hands fall away from him and a frown darkened her brow. This was more than concern for her safety, or perhaps concern hadn't powered his anger as she had thought.

Confused, she headed towards the belt of jungle that divided the clearing from the beach, tightening her sarong over her breasts, bitterly disappointed that he didn't share her euphoria after last night. He followed her and they didn't speak till they were back at the hut.

For the first time Sasha noticed that the storm had torn away most of the flowers Richard had decorated the hut with. They lay all around the clearing, battered and wilted, a bit like her emotions.

Ruefully she set about making coffee, squatting in the corner of the hut to light the bottled-gas ring. He stood leaning on the doorpost, watching her.

'You should have told me, Sasha,' he said softly.

'Since when have I needed your permission to take an early morning swim?'

'I didn't mean that.'

Suddenly she knew what he did mean. 'And your anger manifested itself in the disguise of concern for me swimming in troubled waters, did it?' she scathed back, angry that he should be angry for something most men would have given their eye-teeth for.

'I was worried sick about you when I woke up and found you gone, then when I found you swimming in the sea it angered me more. Yes, I was concerned for your safety but also angry because...because...'

She stood up and faced him, her eyes clouded with her anger.

'Because I seemed so *unconcerned* by what happened last night? Because I wasn't here when you woke up so we could analyse why you were my first lover?'

The sight of him flinching fuelled her anger. 'Yes, you were my first lover and that was my choice, not yours, and if anyone should be angry it should be me, not you, but why on earth did you wait till this morning to show me your disdain? Why didn't you tear me off a strip last night?'

'Stop it, Sasha,' he ordered quietly yet so firmly that she bit her lip. He came towards her and gripped her shoulders and she flinched under his touch. 'Nothing much has changed, has it? We made love last night and yet now you tense under my touch—'

'I have reason to,' she blurted out hotly. 'You're angry with me and you shouldn't be, not if...if you have...have any feelings for me.'

'Dear God, it's because I have feelings for you that you anger me so,' he stated fiercely. 'And I'm angry with myself for my conduct. Call me old-fashioned, call me what the hell you like, but if I had known I wouldn't have pressured you the way I did.'

The blood drained from her face. So this was all a game to him and she had broken the rules. Her mouth worked furiously, bringing the colour back to her face.

'So it would have been all right if you had been my hundredth lover, would it? Now you have a con-science—a misguided conscience. You feel guilty about dropping me now that you've got what you want!'

His grip tightened and his eyes blazed dangerously. 'Yes, I have a conscience and with good reason!' Suddenly his anger fell away from him. His grip softened and he drew her gently into his arms, burying his mouth in her hair.

Sasha didn't struggle. His heart beat furiously against her chest, powered by something more than just anger with her.

'I could have hurt you last night,' he whispered against her. 'I would have liked to have known and I would have been more gentle. I'm angry with myself, not you. I never want to hurt you, Sasha, not ever. You've been hurt enough. I admit I was shocked when we made love. I just assumed . . . well . . . you were engaged to be married and . . .'

She drew back from him slightly and looked up into his face. She tried to smile because she thought she understood. She wanted to explain but it would be so hard.

'Richard,' she breathed softly, 'my . . . my relationship . . . my engagement . . . it wasn't a . . . a love match. I . . . I thought at first it was but something always held me back. I can't really explain what it was—maybe some deep-rooted intuition. I was glad when I found out . . . when I knew he wasn't the right one. I'm doubly glad now.'

Had she said too much? Would he want to know more and so expose her? She didn't want to think along those lines. All she wanted to do was make it right with him. He did care for her—if he didn't he wouldn't have been so upset this morning.

'Does that mean I'm the right one?' he asked, lifting a hand to stroke the side of her face. His eyes were hooded as if suddenly he didn't want that burden of her love hanging about him. Her heart thudded heavily.

How could she admit that in her heart she knew he was the right one? She loved him so very much but perhaps she had been fooling herself in believing that he cared too. She was naïve where love was concerned, had always been naïve where men were concerned. She wanted him to say he loved her now—how naïve could you get?

He said nothing but he held her chin tenderly and lowered his head to brush a kiss across her full lips. She heard the words singing in her mind, though, and convinced herself that he must be thinking them. Maybe she was living in a fool's paradise but for the moment she didn't care.

The wind suddenly raged outside again and a burst of rain lashed in the doorway. Richard drew his mouth from hers and smiled down at her. He kicked the door shut behind him and brushed another kiss across her lips before turning to switch off the gas ring.

'Breakfast can wait,' he said softly, then gathered her to him and drew her down to the cushion of springy ferns.

Sasha lay in his arms, burning with a fever of need that she knew would never die. She didn't know if the future held any hope for them. If she gave herself time to think she'd come up with a painful truth—that because of who she really was they had no future. But the present could not be ignored and she didn't want to think of anything beyond it. The moment was all; she loved him and their relationship, however temporary, had to be made the most of. The future wasn't a consideration.

He eased her sarong from her damp body and mouthed kisses across her breasts, and then looked at her as his hand smoothed down between her thighs. 'Girl Friday,' he whispered, and lowered his head.

She felt his warm lips on her stomach, trailing kisses further and further down, and then she knew an ecstasy that surpassed all others, a delicious sensation of movement as he drew on her and teased her with the tip of his tongue.

His lovemaking was hedonistic, tender yet cruel, a delicious cruelty that teased her to the point of no return. Again and again he brought her back from the edge, again and again she pleaded for mercy, and then her tormentor could hold back no longer himself. He entered her with such desperate intent that she wrapped herself around him, mouthing kisses across his face.

The thatched hut cocooned them in their passion, shielded them from the outside world—a world that Sasha knew she didn't want to face without this man. No, she mustn't think, not now, not now.

She arched against him with a cry of release, gave him her love in a flood of silken passion, and he gave back with a deep moan of ecstasy that drove through her till they clung together, writhing and molten in each other's arms, lost in their passion and exultation.

It rained for the rest of the day, trapping them in their love nest, neither complaining. They opened up the flap window and lay in the ferns watching the skies darken as they ate tropical fruit, feeding each other and laughing and making love till they ached. Sleep when it came was needed and relished as they lay in each other's arms, contented and replete with a deep sense of togetherness.

Never let it end, Sasha breathed to herself over and over again.

'Sun,' Sasha whispered in his ear the next morning.

'Tell it to go away,' Richard muttered wearily, and tried to gather her back into his arms.

She pushed him away, laughing and struggling into her sarong. 'Sun means we can eat outside, make sandcastles on the beach, dive amongst the coral reefs, take a trip in the canoe.'

'And work,' he added ruefully, sitting up and raking his hands through his hair.

Sasha looked down at him, tugging her hair back from her shoulders. They were here to work after all, but the thought of moving off this island didn't fill her with gladness. They had created a world of their own here and she didn't want any outside interference. It was a selfish thought but one she couldn't escape from.

'Do you want to move on?' she asked in a small voice.

He looked up at her, sombre at first, and then his mouth widened into a grin. 'To hell with moving on. You can't top paradise.'

'Is this paradise?' she asked. For her it was; she wondered what he thought of it all.

He stood up, naked and splendid, and cupped her face in his hands. 'It's our paradise. I've never been happier.'

'Nor I,' she whispered, sliding her hands around his waist.

He kissed her tenderly on the lips and her heart squeezed hopelessly. She didn't know why at this moment she should feel that odd pull of hopelessness. She was happy, yes, and he apparently was too, but this was such an unreal situation, a state of time abandoned with no thought of the real world out there. But there was a world beyond paradise and soon it would have to be faced.

Should she tell him now—everything that was her past? A small, inward shudder cast the very thought away. No, she deserved this snatch of happiness; nothing should be allowed to spoil it. When the time came for him to leave she would face her destiny then and only then. And he would have to leave her eventually. She knew something that he didn't—that a future for them was hopeless.

She smiled up at him when they drew apart. 'Promise me you'll never build a drive-in cinema on this spot,' she murmured with laughter in her voice.

'I never make promises I can't keep,' he said with the same inflexion of humour. 'Remember that, Sasha. Never forget it.'

It was funny, but there was no humour in his last words. He'd spoken them with a solemn earnestness that troubled her and yet at the same time filled her with happiness. She didn't understand herself at times.

'Enough is enough!' Sasha cried, exhausted. She ran towards him across the beach, laughing, her hair flying all around her shoulders in the gentle, warm breeze that wafted in from the sea.

She wrested the video camera from his hands. 'I absolutely refuse to be filmed any more. My turn now. Let me film you for a change.' She held it up to her eye. 'OK, action!'

Richard backed away from her, laughing. 'Help, what do I do?'

'You do what you've been making me do for over a week now,' she laughed. 'You can have a taste of your own medicine. Come on, Richard, do a cartwheel or something. Look interesting. You want the people back in Auckland to think this is paradise on earth, don't you?'

A sudden, white-hot flash of panic hit her as she realised what she had said. The camera nearly dropped from her hands and she crumpled down onto the hot sand. Oh, God, why hadn't she thought of that before?

He'd be taking this film back to New Zealand—*all* the film he had shot with her! Nausea wrenched at her stomach and her head came down to her knees.

'Sasha!'

He was beside her in a second, lifting her head and looking at her with such deep concern that she felt worse. She stared at him bleakly, her heart thundering against her ribcage. Love had done this to her, had lifted that impenetrable wall of defence she had built around her after Geoff, leaving her gaping open like a knife-wound. His films would go back to Auckland with him. They could be viewed by people who knew her. Geoff, his very own brother...

'Darling, what's wrong?'

She shook her head, trying to act as if nothing was wrong, but it was all wrong. She could imagine how she looked—distraught because she had just realised that it was all hopeless—her love, her future, this whole stupid paradise.

'It... it's too hot,' she pleaded plaintively. 'Mad dogs and Englishmen and all that.' She struggled to her feet and Richard helped her. She reached for the camera, frantically plotting how she could retrieve and destroy all his film but knowing it was all hopeless. Richard took the camera from her and, with his free arm supporting her, they walked slowly back up the beach.

'You're going to lie down for the rest of the day,' he said tenderly. 'It's all my fault, insisting on cavorting around under this blazing sun. I'm going to look after you and cook you a beautiful meal and...'

'And what?' she questioned meaningfully, the very effort of trying to act with some sort of normality drawing the strength from her bones. A great weariness enveloped her. How could she keep this up? How could she keep the past from him? He must never know and she should never have let all this happen in the first place. How weak she had been, how vulnerable to let him into her heart this way.

'And tomorrow we're leaving,' was all he said.

They reached the thatched hut and wearily Sasha sank down onto the ferns and let the coolness and the shade wash over her.

Richard brought her water and when she lifted her head to sip it she saw the concern for her in his eyes. It tore at her heart and she felt tears coming; she swallowed hard to dispel them.

He did care and she shouldn't have allowed it. She had been selfish in wanting him because some time soon she would have to destroy it all. Once he knew all about her he wouldn't be able to help siding with his brother. He wouldn't believe that she had been the innocent one, disgraced by his brother to save his own skin.

'I mean it. We're leaving tomorrow,' he said quietly as he settled her back against the ferns to rest. 'It might be more than the sun. Malaria is prevalent out here and—'

'And it isn't malaria,' she told him quietly. 'I'm taking all the tablets.

'Richard...' she murmured. His eyes were dark with concern for her as he waited for her to go on. But she had nothing to say; she'd thought she had—she'd thought she wanted to try and explain—but when it came to it she saw the hopelessness of it all and the words lay trapped in her heart. Oh, she loved him so very much but she had to let him go. She'd lived a lie too long to relinquish it now.

'Go on,' he urged tenderly as he smoothed the backs of his fingers down one side of her face.

'It...it doesn't matter,' she murmured. What else was there to say?

'Rest now,' he said, smiling down at her. 'We'll talk later.'

They didn't talk later—not real talk, just small talk as they sat on the veranda watching the sun dip down beyond the jungle and the palm trees. Sasha had picked at her food and Richard had noticed. She had seen him eyeing her plate warily but he hadn't said anything.

'Do you feel up to taking in a few more islands before we go back?' he asked as he lit candles, darkness having swooped down. He came and sat down beside her on the veranda, leaning back on the side of the hut.

She didn't want it to end but knew it must, so why prolong the agony.

'We haven't covered as much as you had anticipated,' she said.

His face was grave in the flickering light of the candles. 'We covered a hell of a lot emotionally.'

'That wasn't the intention, though.'

He sighed deeply. 'No, the object of the exercise was to immerse myself in the islands and come up with some sort of investment plan for tourism.'

'You've changed your mind?'

'Not at all. There's potential here. I'd like to see more but...'

She turned to him. 'But what?'

He lowered his head and picked at a fern, shredding the now fading fronds from the stalk. 'Well, we've had no contact with the outside world for so long now that they might be beginning to worry back at Kula—'

'You mean Henrietta might be fretting for you,' Sasha interjected, and instantly wished she hadn't. She bit her lip to stop any more idiotic things coming out.

'You said that, not me,' he said unnecessarily. 'But—'

'But life goes on,' she whispered.

'Yes, life goes on—yours and mine.'

But in different directions, she wanted to suggest, but didn't because it would have prompted an analysis of what they had been through together and she couldn't face it.

A month, maybe longer, he had said back at Suya, but they hadn't done that month. Had he thought it would take that long to break her down and have his way with her? Oh, no, why was she thinking this way? Time didn't come into it; he had said a month but now he wanted to go back, and it all stemmed from her panic attack on the beach this afternoon. It was as if he knew that something was troubling her.

Suddenly his hand reached out for hers and grasped it so determinedly that she knew something was troubling him too. But she didn't want to expand on that thought so she expelled it and squeezed his fingers.

'Come on,' he said, getting to his feet and drawing her up to hers. 'Let's take a walk before bed.'

It was the very first time he had asked her to join him on his nocturnal ramblings. She said so as they wandered the foaming shoreline, hand in hand under the stars.

He stopped and took her other hand and gazed down at her. 'It's the only time I can really think,' he told her.

'Alone, with no interruptions. I've had a lot on my mind since coming here to the islands—some of it very troublesome, some of it not nice at all, some of it heady stuff.'

Could he have known about her all along? Was this now her punishment for what he believed—rejection? Sasha laughed nervously. 'Sounds serious.'

He smiled. 'You could say that.'

'So... so why ask me to join you now?'

He let go of one hand and lifted her chin. 'Because you are part of my life now,' was all he said before kissing her.

His lips were totally possessive, as was his lovemaking later that night and through the night and into the dawn—totally possessive, as if she were indeed a part of his life for evermore. But in her heart Sasha knew that she never could be, although she couldn't tell him. She was going to have to hurt him very shortly and she didn't know where the strength to do that was going to come from.

It took them an exhausting hour the following morning to pack the two canoes. The sun blazed down and the humidity was severely debilitating; at least, it was to Sasha. Richard worked with the strength of ten men, constantly urging her to take it easy. She ignored his suggestions because while she was working there was no strength left to think.

As Richard secured the last of the packages in the second canoe Sasha wandered back to the clearing. Her eyes were bright with unshed tears as she gazed at the circle of ravaged huts and, in particular, their love hut.

It looked very much the worse for wear after the squall. She could still see it as it was when Richard had transformed it with flowers and ferns and green creeper. It had been the most beautiful sight she had ever seen and what had happened inside had been devastatingly beautiful too.

She stepped closer and gathered a handful of faded flowers from the ground in front of it. She held them in her palm and lifted them to press them against her lips. Then, with a small sob of grief, she lifted her hand and gave the dry petals to the wind, watching as they fluttered and rose and were blown away towards the jungle.

'Saying goodbye?' Richard said from behind her.

She turned to him and forced a smile and nodded.

'Don't you want a souvenir?'

She had one. It was here in her heart, an ache of love.

She watched as he stepped up onto the veranda and then she called out as his hand went up to the sign he had carved out of bark: 'THE LOVE HUT'.

'No, Richard,' she implored. Not that; she wouldn't be able to bear it. 'Leave it; it belongs here and...and you never know...'

He came back to her, his face drawn. 'We might return,' he finished for her.

She smiled and nodded, knowing that they never would. She had been going to say that some other lovers might come here some day, seeking solitude and shelter and a place to love in, but the words wouldn't form because they hurt too much.

'We'd better get moving, then,' she said sensibly. 'We'll have to refuel a couple of times before we hit the home stretch. We'll be pushed to make it in time before nightfall; in fact I think we'll probably have to stop overnight somewhere. No point in pushing the engine to its limits just because...'

Her voice trailed away as he strode past her towards the jungle and the beach and the canoes. She followed, noticing the tenseness of his shoulders as he strode ahead of her, and knew that she had annoyed him with her cold common sense. It had started—the real pain, the real anguish, the real world encroaching.

CHAPTER NINE

THE fates, in the form of good weather, a good wind behind them and prompt refuelling posts, had them back at Suya just before sunset.

'Oh, my legs!' Sasha cried after leaping ashore with relief.

'They look pretty good to me,' Richard joked as he sprang out of the canoe and started hauling it ashore.

Sasha rubbed her calves. 'It's all right for you—you weren't jammed up against all your wretched camera equipment. I couldn't move.'

'Here, let me help.' He knelt down and started massaging her calves for her, gradually working up to her thighs. Sasha slapped his hands playfully and he stopped, smiling up at her and retorting, 'Spoilsport.'

She was glad his humour was back because the trip had been exhausting enough. Hers she'd had to strive for but finally common sense had won over. Every minute was precious with him because any one of them could be the last.

He was staying here tonight with her and going over to Kula later tomorrow and then he had promised to return. He hadn't said what he was going for and she hadn't asked. But it gave her a breathing space and she needed it. She was going to have to let him go and she needed time to come to terms with it and time to work out what to tell him. Should she just tell him the truth and hope that he would believe her? Could she bring herself to tell him that his brother was a liar and a cheat? Oh, God, she didn't know.

'Let's just take the personal stuff in and leave the rest,' he suggested as he hauled out her holdall and his camera gear. 'Do you think it will rain tonight?' he asked as they dragged their weary selves up the beach towards the bungalow.

'I'm not a weather oracle, you know,' she laughed.

'You are. Will it or won't it?'

'It won't.'

'You see, you knew all along.' He pushed open the door and with his body held the bead curtain back for her to go in before him.

'I know one thing,' Sasha said as she brushed past him, her arms weighed down with bags. 'I'm going to stand under that shower for an hour.'

'And I'll join you and massage the bits I missed just now.'

Sasha stopped dead in the sitting room. The bags she was carrying slid to the ground and landed with a thud as she stared in astonishment at Henrietta, sprawled on the wicker sofa.

'Sa...sha!' Richard exclaimed as he nearly tripped over the bags that she had just dropped on the floor. Then his head came up and he saw what had blanched the colour from her face and halted her in her tracks.

'Henrietta! What on earth are you doing here?'

Languidly Henrietta tossed aside the book she was reading as if it were a piece of trash. Her venomous eyes gave Sasha the same treatment as they washed over her from head to toe. Travel-weary, dirty and unkempt, her hair ravaged by the sea breeze, Sasha knew that she looked her worst. And Richard didn't look much better.

Henrietta eyed them both with the same blatant disdain. Slowly she swung her legs down from the sofa and got to her feet.

She looked directly at Sasha, her eyes piercing and hateful. 'Disappear, will you? I have things to discuss with Richard,' she clipped out tightly.

Sasha's eyes widened. 'Excuse me!' she blazed. 'This is my home and it's not for you to tell me what to do—'

'Sasha, don't,' Richard cut in, dropping his camera equipment to the floor. 'What's this all about, Henrietta?'

'Just a minute, Richard,' she said coolly, subjecting him to an equally chilling glare. She turned her icy eyes to Sasha again. 'Let me remind you that this is my uncle's house and if my uncle dropped dead tomorrow, which incidentally is quite likely after what you have put him through, this property would be mine, and if I had my way I'd have you out of here and off these islands before you had the chance to reason why.'

Appalled, Sasha felt her mouth drop open. Confusion swamped her till she felt dizzy with it.

'Stop it, Henrietta,' Richard thundered. 'What the hell has got into you?'

'You'll find out in a minute,' she sparked back. 'When I'm ready and when that filthy wretch has taken herself off to the shower. *Alone*,' she added pointedly, which meant that she had overheard Richard's joky remark about joining Sasha there. Was that what this was all about—a 'woman scorned' routine?

'I'll shower when I'm good and ready,' Sasha retorted, finding her voice at last.

Richard was eyeing Henrietta dangerously and for a second Sasha was grateful for his support, but then the world crashed in on her as slowly he said, 'It might be a good idea if you did as Henrietta suggested, Sasha.'

'No way!' she seethed. 'I don't take orders from her, or you, come to that. Not in my own home.'

She stormed into the kitchen, snatched at the coffee-jug with fingers that trembled, and realised in that moment that the kitchen wasn't the way she had left it—neat and tidy ready for their return.

'Just how long have you been here?' she raged at Henrietta from the doorway.

Henrietta gave her a supercilious look that would have put down a lesser person.

'Two days. Two days of hell in this dump—'

'Henrietta, will you stop this and tell us what is going on?' Richard interjected firmly. 'Sasha is right; this is her home and she has a right to know why you are here. It's obvious you have some sort of grievance with me, not her, so cut out the spiteful remarks and get on with it. Start with explaining why you are here and not waiting for me back at Kula.'

Clenching her fists as her sides, Henrietta seethed, 'I'm here because I knew it would be the first place you'd come back to. We've had no contact with you since you left and my uncle is furious, as it happens, and—'

'Is that what this is about?' Richard said scornfully, his dark brows drawn down over his furious eyes. 'Since when have I had to answer to the two of you?'

Henrietta was momentarily perplexed by his outburst but then recovered. Her lips tightened furiously.

Sasha shifted uncomfortably. She didn't want to hear all this. Their spiteful jabs at each other were nothing

to do with her. She went to cross the room to her
bedroom to take that shower. To hell with them, she
thought.

Henrietta caught her arm and stopped her. 'You might
as well stay, seeing as this is all about you anyway.' She
turned her furious eyes back to Richard. 'You know what
this is about, Richard, don't you?' She didn't give him
a chance to answer but ploughed spitefully on. 'You're
finished on these islands as far as your damned investment plans go, and she's finished too now that my
uncle knows what he does and—'

'Sasha, leave us,' Richard suddenly ordered gravely.
His hand came up and raked through his hair, and Sasha
watched him, wide-eyed.

A terrible fear started to run up from the base of her
spine. Richard knew what Henrietta was going on about
and...and he looked guilty about it. Oh, God, what
was going on? She opened her mouth to ask but the
wicked smile on Henrietta's lips stilled the words in her
throat.

'"Sasha, leave us,"' she mimicked cruelly, her pale
eyes holding Sasha's for impact. 'Don't you mean
Letitia, leave us?'

Sasha heard a soft moan of resignation from Richard
and then her blood roared in her ears, the noise so deaf-
ening that it drowned out the soft tinkling of Henrietta's
laugh of triumph. So this was it. She knew; this awful
woman knew and she was going to be the one to tell
Richard.

Oh, what a fool she had been to think she could have
kept it from him. But she had considered telling him and
now it was too late. Her legs worked automatically,

powering her towards the sanctuary of her bedroom. She had to get away; she couldn't face either of them.

Richard caught her this time and swung her into his arms, holding her tightly as if he was never going to let her go.

'It's all right, darling,' he soothed. 'It's all right.'

Sasha clung to him, knowing that it wasn't all right. It was all so horribly wrong.

'Very touching,' Henrietta simpered sarcastically. 'You're a damned good actor, Richard, I'll say that for you. Was that your plan all along—to seduce her back to civilisation? Was that what her father hired you for—?'

'Shut up!' Richard roared, his whole body trembling with rage against Sasha's heated body.

Sasha thought the end of the world had come. Her whole body stiffened painfully as Henrietta's accusations sank in. Her head dropped back and she looked up at him with glazed eyes, her heart racing so fast and so hard that she thought it would burst.

'You ... you knew,' she whispered hoarsely.

He looked down at her, eyes full of pain and hurt, arms still holding her against him. 'Yes, my darling, I knew.'

The end of her world *had* come. Her body went limp; her heart was giving out. The fists that had clawed at Richard's shirt for support unfolded painfully and she drew back from him, pushing at him, wanting him and that Hun out of her space.

The fury rose then and she hit at him, pounding her small fists on his chest. He took the punishment, did nothing to stop her. She thumped his chest, sobbing all the while deep, heart-rending cries of pure pain for what he had done to her. He didn't love her; he didn't care one bit. She hated him!

At last her strength gave out and Richard was there for her. He took hold of her shuddering shoulders and eased her into the nearest chair where she slumped pitifully, dropping her head into her hands and sobbing her heart out.

Richard moved to the kitchen, came back with a glass of water and forced her to take some.

'Satisfied now, Henrietta?' he bit out without turning to look at her, concentrating on Sasha, who clasped the glass tightly in her white hands.

'It's all she deserved,' Henrietta said, slightly subdued but not for long. 'She's a damned drug addict, a whore for running off with a man old enough to be her father. She nearly wrecked your brother's life—'

'I didn't!' screamed Sasha, her strength back, her anger filling the room. 'I did none of those things, none of them!'

'Stop it, both of you!' Richard ordered firmly. There was no anger in him now, just a calmness that was far more effective than thundering orders. He turned to Henrietta who had slumped back down onto the cane sofa. 'You have some explaining to do, Henrietta. How did you know all this? Where did you get your rubbishy information from?'

'It's not rubbish, it's the truth, as you well know.' She fumbled in her bag, drew out a letter and handed it to Richard who had to step towards her to take it from her.

Sasha's head jerked up to see what was going on. She recognised the envelope immediately, and the stamps and the writing. The letter had been opened.

'That's my letter!' she cried. 'From my father!'

'It's not for you, Sasha,' Richard said quietly. 'It's addressed to me.' Before she could protest he said to Henrietta, 'How dare you open my mail?'

'You weren't there,' she retorted. 'I thought it might be important and opened it and it's a damned good job I did. As you can see, it doesn't tell the whole story but it hints at enough. I remembered the scandal from way back and had no idea Letitia McKenzie was who she is now. The letter aroused my curiosity so I got in touch with friends in Auckland—important, influential friends—and it was easy to find out more about this lying bitch.'

She fumbled in her bag again and came out with another envelope, crammed full of old press cuttings. Sasha couldn't bear to look and lowered her swimming head.

'You had no right,' Richard breathed tightly. He waved the press cuttings away dismissively. 'I don't want to see that garbage.'

'No, because you've seen it all before. You knew what she had put Geoff through—your very own brother— yet you agreed to come out here for her father and persuade her to go back to Auckland. You used me and my uncle to get you out here, and for what? That little tramp! Where the hell do your loyalties lie, Richard?'

There was a long, long silence in the room. Outside, the sea shushed over the coral reef, the cicadas buzzed. Life went on out there but life stood still in the bungalow. It was dark now and only one light burned, next to Henrietta on the sofa. Sasha lifted her head to look at it because it was unbearable to look at either of these people. At last the silence was broken by Richard.

'Well, you've certainly brought me down to earth, Henrietta,' he said softly. 'So you shall be the first to know. My loyalties lie with the woman I love and am going to marry.'

Sasha's heart broke then. She might have known that it was all hopeless. He had lied to her, deceived her, made her love him and now he was going to marry Henrietta!

She felt a soft caress on the top of her hand and her head jerked up, rebelling at the patronising touch of his fingers on her hair. Her heart lurched as he looked down at her with such deep love in his eyes that her spirits soared. But not for long. Punch-drunk by the verbal blows that had been dealt her, she couldn't reason that the look of love was genuine.

She moved then, in jerky, uncoordinated movements that propelled her from the chair and rushed her to her bedroom. No one tried to stop her. She slammed the door behind her, put her hand to her heart and let out a silent sob of despair.

How could she believe anyone any more? How had she ever put her love and trust in him? He was just like his brother… Oh, worse than his brother…he had *made* her love him.

Shakily she turned the shower full on to drown out the murmur of voices in the next room. Not harsh voices now. They would resolve their differences, blow her out of their world and she would have to start all over again. Somewhere, somehow.

He came to her later—much later. He brought her hot coffee and a meal. She was curled up on her bed, clutching at her shoulders, shivering in spite of the oppressive heat. She turned to him.

'Take that away! I'd choke on anything *she* cooked!'

'I cooked it,' he told her, sitting on the edge of the bed, holding the plate on his lap. 'Rice and meat sauce—canned, I'm afraid, but the best I could do under the circumstances.'

'Has she gone?' she asked hopefully.

'No, she's gone to bed in my room.'

'And no doubt you will be joining her!' It was a pitiful thing to say but she didn't really know what she was saying any more.

Richard ignored the suggestion. 'She can't go tonight. One of her uncle's boys brought her over and left her here, and I'm in no fit state to unload our canoe to take her back in the dark. I'll take her first thing in the morning and then I'll be back.'

'What for? To torment me some more? Don't bother! I never want to see you again in my life!'

'But *I* want to see *you*,' he said authoritatively. 'And, as you well know, I always get what I want.'

Sasha's lips tightened. Oh, yes, he always got what he wanted, hearts and souls.

'Here, try this. It's not half bad.' He forked up the rice and held it to her lips. She turned away from him and curled up in a ball again.

He sighed. 'At least drink the coffee, Sasha—'

'Don't you mean Letitia?' she uttered sarcastically.

She felt the pressure go from the bed and then he smoothed his fingers across her brow. 'What's in a name? I'd love you whatever you were called.'

She heard the door click shut behind him and squeezed shut her eyes, balling her hands into small fists. Liar! Liar! she screamed silently.

* * *

She was up at dawn. Though she had slept eventually, falling into an exhausted unconsciousness, she didn't feel refreshed. Her head throbbed and she'd forgotten the mosquito net and her legs had been bitten. She slipped on a bikini.

'Where are you going?'

Richard was on the sofa, the chair pulled up to give an extension for his long legs. He hauled himself up to face her. She only briefly felt relief at the fact that he had slept there all night.

'I'm going for a swim. Do you think I should ask the Hun's permission first?' she asked bitingly.

'Who's the Hun?' came a sleepy query from the other bedroom door. Henrietta stood there, draped in pale blue satin trimmed with ostrich feathers that wafted as she spoke.

'Look in the mirror,' Sasha retorted, and strode out of the room.

She swam till she ached and then swam some more. Eventually she conceded defeat and strolled wearily back up to the bungalow, passing Richard unloading the canoe as she went. Neither spoke.

Henrietta was sipping coffee on the veranda. Dressed and refreshed, she looked coolly elegant in a natural linen skirt with matching blouse. She looked very out of place. The veranda was shabby, the sun-bleached wooden bungalow in need of some refurbishing. It was the first time that Sasha had noticed.

Henrietta surveyed her with disdain. 'The end of the world wouldn't have been far enough for you to run,' she said bitterly as Sasha came up the steps.

'Yes, you're right, not nearly far enough,' Sasha stated wearily, pausing to look down at her enemy. 'If I'd thought people like you still graced the earth I would have kept on running.'

Henrietta afforded her a cynical smile. 'You can't go back, you know.' She nodded towards Richard, who was still on the beach by the canoes. 'He can't help you. He thinks he's in love with you but he's not. He feels sorry for you and is using you as a weapon against his father, who favours Geoff. You're a pathetic pawn in their power games, that's all.

'You're finished here too. A junkie running a hospital with access to a pharmacy—my uncle is writhing at the thought.' She turned to Sasha and smiled sweetly at her. 'Where to now, Letitia? You're running out of places to bolt to.'

Sasha knew in that moment that she should never have run in the first place. Nothing had been gained by it and nothing would be gained if she ran once more.

But did she have the strength to go back and face her family? If she ever found it she would have to do it alone. Henrietta's torturous revelations were powered by jealousy but there was a lot of truth in what she said. Richard couldn't help her even if he wanted to.

She said nothing to the bitter woman who was waiting for her answer, probably ready with a few more insults on the tip of her waspish tongue. She wouldn't waste her breath on her. Henrietta believed what she believed and nothing would change it. Sasha didn't have to protest her innocence; she knew in her heart that she was guilt-free. She felt sorry for Henrietta more than anything. Henrietta hadn't had the Love Hut, hadn't had Richard's passion, hadn't had the laughter and the fun. Powered by pity or whatever, he had nevertheless changed her world.

She was making fresh coffee after dressing and brushing out her hair when Richard came into the small kitchen.

'I don't know how long this will take but I'll be back as soon as possible.'

He didn't make any attempt to touch her and she was glad. She would have crumbled if he had.

'Don't feel obliged to come back,' she told him without looking at him. 'I'll understand if you don't.'

'I'm coming back, Sasha,' he stated determinedly. 'We have to talk.'

She looked at him then. 'Don't you think enough has been said already?'

'Not nearly enough,' he said roughly. 'You haven't heard my side of all this yet.'

Her eyes narrowed painfully. 'Oh, you have a side, do you? I thought all this was hit-Sasha-below-the-belt week? If you do come back, Richard, don't expect any compassion from me. I'm the injured party, not you or Lady Pitiful out there, waiting for you. I've suffered enough at the hands of your family and I suspect there's plenty more where that came from.'

She nodded towards the veranda. 'You can thank her for me, actually; she's done me one big favour—strengthened the reasons why I ran in the first place. There are hundreds more like her waiting back in—'

'Will you stop this self-pity, Sasha?' he flashed suddenly. 'It doesn't suit you and it isn't you. A handful of your past thrown at you and you're going under. Fight it, Sasha, starting now, because you're going to need the practice. You're going to have to fight for your very existence when we get back to Auckland—'

'Go back?' she croaked, already backtracking on her original plans. 'Why the—?'

'Leave it, Sasha,' he warned darkly. 'Leave it till I get back because this isn't the time. The time is later, when we are on our own—'

'Go to hell!' she blazed.

'I've already been, there and back, and I've no intentions of making a further visit. Now lighten up because this isn't the tragedy you think it is. You're not on your own. You have me now and I'm with you all the way.'

'And that's supposed to inspire me with confidence, is it?' she cried then. 'Don't walk away from me when I'm shouting at you...Richard!'

Sasha ran after him, and stopped on the veranda when she saw the look of triumph on Henrietta's face as she waited for him on the beach. She must have heard it all, heard the panic in her voice. She must have heard Richard's reassurances too, but once she had him away from her she was satisfied that she could make him see the light.

And she'd do her best to blacken Sasha's name further, with the help of her uncle, no doubt. Richard was a Carlton, after all, and none of them turned a blind eye to a good investment proposition. John Harvey, with the aid of his irascible niece, would grind her into the ground rather than let Richard return to her and Richard would accept that because, as the Hun had said, it was all a power game.

She watched them depart, Henrietta sitting bolt upright with that smirk still on her face, Richard with his back to her as he guided the canoe through the tricky reef. Sasha felt a despair like no other she had ever experienced. She had lost him.

CHAPTER TEN

SASHA powered her despair into hauling all the gear they had taken on their trip back up the beach to the bungalow. In his haste to get away with Henrietta Richard had dumped it on the hot sand. Most of it was his so he would have to return.

She ate a light lunch on the veranda because she would need her strength later when he came back. Afterwards she rested for an hour and tried to sleep but it was impossible. Eventually she got up and started cleaning the bungalow. Henrietta had been here for two days and obviously kept slaves back in New Zealand because she hadn't cleaned up after her.

She would have to vacate the bungalow and her beloved sanctuary, of course. John Harvey wouldn't allow her to stay. He'd probably see to it that she never worked anywhere in the islands again. So where would she go? She had absolutely no idea.

She couldn't bear to trudge through the jungle to see her secret place for the last time. It would hurt too much. She couldn't bear to paddle out to sea and say goodbye to the dolphins either. It was all spoiled now. Nothing would ever be the same again.

She waited in the shade of the veranda, waited and waited till she heard the familiar drone of the outboard in the distance. It was late afternoon and the day had felt a year long.

She stood up as he approached, her sunshine-yellow pareu wafting and her hair gently waving in the warm breeze. She loved him; she still loved him and always would but he had betrayed her. He had always known who she was and he had never let on, and whatever he had to say to her now she would never forgive him for making her love him.

'So you haven't taken flight,' he said as he came onto the veranda.

Sasha sat down on a wicker chair. 'That's a silly thing to say as I'm here.'

He shrugged, sat down on the other chair and reached for the jug of juice on the table. 'I didn't know what else to say to open it all up. If I'd swept you into my arms and proclaimed my undying love you wouldn't have believed me.'

'True,' she murmured, lowering her head to pick at the seam of her pareu.

'I do love you, Sasha, passionately, from the moment I first set eyes on you,' he said tenderly.

'Passion with intent,' she uttered weakly. She raised her green eyes to meet his. 'And how many pieces of gold passed hands between you and my father to buy that passion, Richard?'

She saw a flash of anger in his eyes. 'What an absurd question.'

'Is it? I think not. My father sent you, didn't he?'

'No one makes me do anything I don't want to do. I was coming here anyway. The tourist plan is genuine, not a ploy to get you away from here to seduce you as you think. You were a coincidence, Sasha.'

'Some creaking coincidence, eh?' she said sceptically. 'That's hard to swallow.'

'It's the truth. You really were a coincidence. Now I'm going to tell you everything, and I want you to listen and try and understand my side of all this. Will you?'

She nodded.

'If you remember, I was coming back from South America for your marriage to my brother. What I found on my return was pandemonium. You'd done a runner, the wedding was off, the family were in a state of chaos, and Geoff was running around as if his tail was on fire.'

'Panic,' Sasha mumbled, but Richard didn't hear and went on.

'I stayed and helped the best I could. Geoff made accusations against you and the Press made a meal of the whole mess.'

'And . . . and you believed it all,' Sasha said weakly. 'And you were still believing it when you met me here. You were horrible to me in the beginning—scathing and—'

'I didn't believe it or disbelieve it; it wasn't an issue for me. But put yourself in my shoes. Of course I suffered suspicious thoughts; who wouldn't against all the damning evidence?'

'No smoke without fire,' Sasha bit out.

'Exactly. There is always room for doubt and when I first met you you were hardly sweetness and light. There you were, all spiky and proud, stuffed full of confidence, with a smart mouth. Yes, I gave you a hard time till I realised you weren't what I had been led to believe. But two years ago I didn't know you and passed no judgements. My main concern was stabilising the family after the scandal.'

'Which you did, of course, arranging *another* suitable marriage for your brother,' she breathed sarcastically.

'Not at all. This time it was a love match for him.'

Sasha winced and drew her arms about her.

'I'm sorry,' he offered tenderly, leaning towards her. 'That wasn't meant to hurt you, Sasha, but it's the truth. You were ill matched with my brother and you realised that yourself—you told me.'

She nodded bleakly and he went on, 'As far as Geoff was concerned I soon realised there was more to it than met the eye. No man who truly loved a woman could say the things he did about you after you left. Putting anger and rejection aside, he couldn't have said what he did if he'd had love and respect for you.'

'So... so you thought there was more to it?' she asked hesitantly and a little hopefully.

'I suspected the marriage had been arranged and hadn't been a true love match for my brother. It was a passing thought but not one I gave much thought to at the time. Don't forget, I didn't know you but I do know my own brother and—'

'And blood is thicker than water.'

Richard leaned back in his chair. 'I didn't side with him, if that's what you think. It really wasn't any of my concern at the time.'

'So why the concern now?' she bit back.

'I had business with your father—'

'You said you didn't know my father, said you'd never heard of him,' Sasha protested hotly.

'I said I'd never heard of a banker by the name of Thompson, remember?'

'Y-yes,' she murmured, and rubbed her forehead fretfully. 'Nevertheless you deceived me all along, Richard. All the time I was giving you snippets of my past you knew it all. I told you things I've never told anyone before and all the time you knew. Sometimes you said things that made me think you did know who I was but then you glossed over it so that I was uncertain.'

Her anger started to bubble. 'And then...then I trusted you, loved you. You took advantage of me, made love to me, used me all the way. I suppose you believed all those lies about me, thought you were on to a good thing and—'

'Stop it, Sasha, just stop it!' he ordered firmly.

She bit her lip and clenched her fingers in her lap. 'Go on, then. Get it off your chest, salve your conscience, appease the gods...' She let out a deep sigh. 'I'm sorry, go on.'

'I had business with your father,' he repeated. 'At first he was wary of me, being a Carlton, but he learned to trust me and we became friends. It didn't take me long to realise how deeply he felt for you and how badly he had been shaken by the whole business.

'You know your father well enough. As a banker he's one of the best; all his energies go into his work at the expense of human relationships and emotions. As a father and a husband he's all at sea. Your stepmother dominates him on the home front and he didn't know how to handle his emotions over you running away the way you did.'

'I know,' she breathed mournfully. Her father wouldn't have understood if she had told him the true story, and once she had gone the gulf had widened even more.

'I told him my plans to come out to the Solomon Islands—nothing to do with you,' he insisted, 'because I didn't know you were here. It was then that he opened up to me more. He told me where you were, the name you were living under. This was where the enormous co-incidence came in. I was already dealing with John Harvey; your father didn't know that but he pleaded with me to look you up, to somehow try and talk some sense into you. He wants you back, Sasha.'

Sasha sat staring down at her clenched fingers. And she wanted to go back. She hadn't before Richard had come. She had felt safe here but, thanks to him and Henrietta, had discovered that you couldn't run far enough in this world. She wanted to see her father; she missed him and wanted to make it good with him. She had put him through so much.

'And . . . and Henrietta—where did she come in when you planned this trip?'

'She wanted to visit her uncle, that's all.'

'Another coincidence—the fact that John was her uncle and you just happened to be paying him a visit? Huh!'

Richard gave her a small smile. 'Maybe she had designs on me and saw the opportunity of having her way with me *en route*. I honestly don't know and don't care. Henrietta is a survivor. It's you I love—from that first moment when I hauled you into that old trader.'

Her eyes narrowed at him. 'Am I expected to believe that, Richard?'

'It's the truth.'

'I'm not that gullible,' she said with disdain. 'You would *supposedly* have fallen in love with me at John Harvey's party when you found out who I was, because that was your plan—the only way you thought you could get me back to my father, the *easiest* way. As I said, passion with intent!'

She pushed her chair back and got up. 'Like all the Carltons, Richard, you lack any sort of credibility. I don't believe a word you say. You knew who I was from the start, probably when you hauled me aboard, and you did what you had to do.'

She turned away, her heart tight in her chest, and went to step off the veranda and walk away from him, as far as was possible on this tiny tropical island.

'Haven't you forgotten something?' he drawled. He stretched out lazily in his chair, not making any attempt to get up and follow her to wherever.

Sasha stopped and looked across at the sun dipping into the sea. It would be dark shortly. She turned her face back to him.

'Yes, of course—goodnight!'

'Sasha!' he called out as she headed for the shoreline where the cool of the water would salve her aching senses. She stopped again, turning slightly. He was leaning on the veranda rail.

'You forget something quite important, something quite relevant under the circumstances.' He let his words hang there in the still, hot air, tempting her to question what he meant.

She obliged. 'Oh, yes, and what is that?'

'The small detail that you knew exactly who I was from the start too—the brother of the man you jilted...'

Her fists balled at her sides and she took a sharp breath, then her heart tipped painfully as he went on, 'You allowed what happened between us, Sasha, knowing who I was all the time you were loving me. Which way do I take that? I'll give you two choices— you couldn't help yourself because you fell in love with me, or you *are* the tramp my brother made you out to be. Take your pick!'

Her eyes filled with a sudden rush of tears. How could he be so cruel? She was tempted to pick the latter and then he would be out of her life for ever, but pride rallied. Damn the Carltons; she wasn't going to take any more from them, not any of them. So, admit her love for him? Not with her last breath would she give him that satisfaction.

'You'll never know,' she called out, and, turning her back on him, she carried on walking.

She came back to the bungalow much later, not at all refreshed, her brain exhausted from wrestling with her emotions. She didn't want him here because all the while he stayed he was making it more painful for her. The lights burned in the bungalow and there was a smell of coffee brewing and he . . . he was fiddling around with his video player!

'What are you doing?' she clipped, stopping in the sitting room, not able to believe that he was more concerned with the films he'd taken on their trip than with her.

'I'm going to prove a point,' he mumbled as he switched on the television.

'What—that your trip wasn't entirely wasted and you'll make money out of these islands regardless of what you've put me through?' she said bitterly.

'Stop feeling sorry for yourself, Sasha. Bring the coffee through and sit down and watch this.'

She lifted her chin. 'I'm not interested—'

'But I am,' he told her curtly, turning to look at her, his dark eyes grave. 'Stop fighting me, Sasha. I've no intention of putting you down—'

'Oh, no? The road to hell is paved with good intentions—'

He was on his feet in a split-second and angry with it.

'OK!' she stormed. 'I'll get the coffee and I'll watch your silly films and then you can go. Bargain?'

'I bargain with no one and if—'

She held her hands up in defeat. 'OK, OK, I'm on my way.' She hurried to the kitchen and came back a minute later with the coffee. She poured two cups, sat on the sofa and stared blankly at the screen.

'Watch yourself carefully, Sasha. A sharp lady like you should be able to spot the point I'm trying to make.'

He came and sat next to her on the sofa and she shifted away slightly, so acutely aware of the heat of his body that she felt it to be a punishment.

'I'm obviously not as smart as you think I am,' she muttered, 'because I really don't see the object of the exercise.'

'You will when you see yourself on screen. The camera doesn't lie, Sasha; remember that.'

And she knew exactly what he meant when she saw herself. It flooded through her like a tidal wave. It was there to see in her laughter, in her eyes, in the glow of her skin. Sasha swimming, Sasha laughing, Sasha running towards her lover on the beach, Sasha cooking on the open fire outside the Love Hut. Sasha *in love*.

'So you see,' he murmured quietly, ejecting the film, 'you can't deny it. You're a woman in love.'

Sasha sighed hopelessly and leaned back, cradling her coffee-cup in her hands. 'And not that other label your brother branded me with and you accused me of being,' she whispered meekly.

'After getting to know you I knew for sure you couldn't have been capable of any of those things,' he told her softly. 'I said what I did earlier to try and jolt you into admitting you did love me and into voicing some sort of denial of all that was said against you.'

He took the cup from her fingers and, putting it down with his on the coffee-table, sat down next to her. He turned her towards him and held her hands.

'I want you to tell me everything, Sasha—everything that happened to you to cause you to take flight two years ago.'

She pulled her hands from his instantly and stood up, her eyes wide with pain as she looked down at him.

'Why?' she pleaded. 'What has it got to do with now? You found me; you made me love you; you can go back and report to my father that I'm alive and well and human again; so why the need to know any more?'

He sighed and leaned forward, raking his hands through his hair, and when he spoke she suspected that he was losing patience with her.

He looked up at her and said slowly and meaningfully, 'Sasha, you are going to have to tell your father yourself because that's the only way. I'm taking you back to Auckland—'

'I'm not going back,' she stated urgently, wringing her hands as she spoke. 'And you making ridiculous suggestions about marrying me is just a ploy to get me back. If you really cared for me you'd leave me alone—'

'It's just because I do care that I'm still here.' He stood up, touched her chin, pushed her hair back from her troubled face and smoothed warm, reassuring fingers down her cheek. She let him because her heart told her that she wanted it to be all right, but her senses told her it never could be. 'I could do all you say, Sasha—leave you here and report back to your father—but that isn't the right way and I can't do it.'

'Because you feel sorry for me and—'

'No, because I love you and want you and can't imagine my life without you,' he said fervently. 'I know you love me too because you couldn't have allowed it all to happen after all you've been through, and knowing who I was as well, if you didn't. I've put you through another form of hell, pushing you the way I have, making you love me, wanting to draw you out of your shell and—'

'And that was selfish of you!'

'Yes, it was selfish,' he admitted. 'I won you and I couldn't have done if you hadn't felt the same way. Now you're fighting me because you think I've betrayed you. There was no plan to seduce you for any other reason than I fell in love with you and wanted you.'

She looked up at him, wanting to believe him so badly, seeing reassurance and love and hope in his eyes and yet feeling hopelessly inadequate to cope with it.

He slid his arms around her and drew her close, dropping small kisses on the top of her head. Then he lifted her chin and kissed her tenderly, and it was all that was needed to open the floodgates of her heart and let out all the hopelessness she had gathered inside her.

She pushed him away, fled to her bedroom and flung herself down on the bed, sobbing uncontrollably.

She felt his weight on the edge of the bed as he sat down. He touched her shoulder lightly and she tightened herself into a ball.

'I'm not leaving, Sasha; you must believe—'

'I do believe you!' she blurted out suddenly, and rolled over to face him. 'But that isn't the end of it, is it? Henrietta was right—'

'What has she said to you?' He hauled her up to a sitting position and his eyes were bright with anger.

Suddenly Sasha was angry too, and bitter. 'The truth, Richard; she pointed out the very truth that you couldn't help me . . . you were just playing power . . . power games with your family—'

'Ridiculous!' he cried, clutching at her shoulders.

'Is it ridiculous? It's what your brother did to me— wanted to marry me to please his father because it would have been a good business move to merge the two families.'

'So you think I want to marry you for the same reason?' he exploded.

'No, I don't . . . I don't. It goes deeper than that. Oh, God,' she wailed and lowered her head to his shoulder. 'I can't think straight.' She swallowed hard and lifted her head, trying to get it right in her mind.

'When . . . when Henrietta mentioned power games I was so angry and hurt that I believed it, but then I didn't because I know you're different from them. You have nothing to gain from marrying me because you are your own person. But can't you see how impossible it all will be?'

He shook his head. 'Not impossible, darling—difficult but not impossible.'

Her eyes widened appealingly. 'Richard,' she said softly, 'just now you asked me to tell you all that happened two years ago. If I did I would be telling you things about your brother that you just won't want to hear, that you might not even believe because he is your very own brother.'

He held her trembling shoulders steady and looked deep into her troubled green eyes. 'The drugs and the women, you mean?' he whispered.

A small gasp escaped her lips and she went weak in his arms, and then he was holding her tightly and lovingly and she clung to him, fresh tears flooding from her eyes.

'Oh, God, you know,' she sobbed.

'Not everything, my darling,' was all he said.

'It..it was why I ran,' she cried. 'The...the day before the wedding...I found him with a woman...drugs... They were doing drugs and I...I was so sick...and horrified...'

He eased her back from him, brushing the tears from her flushed face. 'You ran,' he murmured, looking deep into her eyes with such love and understanding that she felt hope creep back into her muddled senses.

She swallowed hard, battling to stop the distress that was threatening to overwhelm her. 'He...Geoff...he caught me at the door. He said it was nothing and that everyone did it. Then he said awful things about the marriage having to go ahead because of his father.

'I...I couldn't speak I was so shocked. I think it made him realise just what he had done. He started threatening me then, said if I told anyone he'd ruin me and my father. I...I didn't know which way to turn...I didn't know what to do...' A sob caught in her throat.

'So you ran.' Richard's voice was thick with emotion.

Sasha nodded and looked up at him, her eyes swimming. 'I panicked,' she whispered. 'I couldn't tell my family. My stepmother was so determined about the wedding that she would never have believed a word said against Geoff. And my father...' She sighed deeply. 'He was always so busy with his work. I just didn't know how he would react. I just wanted to run, to get away from it all.'

'Is this where the friend of your father came in?'

'Yes. He lived close to Geoff's apartment and he'd always seemed such a nice man to me. I knew he was going to Singapore on business. Oh, it was just a spur-of-the-moment thing. I went to him, not knowing where else to go. It was stupid of me but I just needed someone to lean on till I could collect my senses. I...I told him I'd had second thoughts about the wedding...

'Oh, God,' she cried and lowered her head, not able to meet his eyes, feeling such a fool about how gullible she had been.

'Go on, darling,' he urged, the caring note in his voice giving her strength.

She shook her head. She'd never been able to come to terms with her stupidity and blindness over Don Hertz.

'He...he suggested I join him on his business trip, to cool down and reconsider my future with Geoff. I knew I had no future with him but I was afraid to stay, afraid Geoff would get to me and persuade me to go through with the wedding. I was also afraid that if I stayed I might blurt out the truth and Geoff would damage my father in some way.

'So, like a fool, I agreed to go with Don, seeing him as a means of escape. I didn't really think about it seriously, just agreed in a panic. I didn't realise what I was doing. We got to Singapore and...and he booked us in at the hotel as man and wife. I couldn't believe it—couldn't believe I hadn't seen it coming.'

His hands on her shoulders were caressing her. 'So you ran again?' he prompted.

She nodded. 'I ended up in a cheap hotel, running out of money and as desperate as I'd been when I left Auckland, and with the same threats ringing in my ears from Don Hertz.

'The Press had a field-day. Geoff must have thought that when I'd run there was a good chance I'd reveal what I'd found out about him. I wouldn't have done that; it was such a horrible shock that I couldn't have spoken to anyone about it. He did what he did out of self-preservation, I suppose—made me out to be a flighty, spoilt bitch, experimenting with drugs. Same with Don Hertz—a man scorned.'

She sighed deeply. 'I managed to get this job out here, changed my name, told a few lies. I'm sorry John found out and believed ill of me—'

'He doesn't, Sasha. I talked with him earlier and he understands,' Richard told her quietly.

Sasha's eyes widened. 'But Henrietta said—'

'Henrietta said a lot in the heat of the moment. Yes, he was shocked, but you've done a lot for the hospital and he realises that, and I put him right on a few things.'

'So he doesn't think as Henrietta does?'

'No, he doesn't. He's a good judge of character and he understands that something must have driven you to change your identity and escape here to the islands.

'I had a long talk with Henrietta as well. Of course I couldn't tell her what you've just told me because I didn't know, and even if I had I wouldn't. Her second cousin is married to Geoff and I'm not into wrecking marriages. Besides, Geoff has mended his ways and is a good and dutiful husband to her. I think you had something to do with that.'

She looked puzzled. 'How do you mean?'

'You obviously frightened him out of his ways. He's a stronger, better person now.'

Sasha smiled ruefully. 'I did him good and he did me nothing but bad.'

'I think he made a strong woman out of you, Sasha. Look what you've achieved—so much against the odds. You fought and you won.'

'Huh, what have I won? I've got no job, nowhere to go—'

'You still have a job here, and a home; John is adamant about that but you won't need either of them. You have me,' he said warmly, 'and a father waiting for you at home, and a stepmother who has mellowed with time and will be only too happy to arrange the wedding of her stepdaughter to another Carlton—this time to the elder Carlton who has a ton more money than any of them,' he teased.

'Oh, Richard,' she laughed, but there was still tears in her eyes. 'Money doesn't matter.' She grew serious again. 'I...I can't marry you. I can't face them back home and—'

'You can and you will,' he said earnestly. 'You owe it to yourself. It's started already, with John Harvey. He didn't take much persuading that you're a good person; he already knew that. What happened two years ago is history now. People will have forgotten. The Press won't hassle you, I'll see to that. I'll love and protect you and no one will dare broach the subject ever again.'

His mouth suddenly closed over hers and it was as if that kiss held all the answers in the world—a soft, reassuring pressure on her mouth that said so much, that said it would be all right and together they would weather any storm that came their way.

She clung to him, wishing it could happen, willing herself to believe that with this wonderful man at her side she could face an army and win the war that she would have to face if she agreed to go back with him.

'Oh, Richard,' she murmured passionately against him. 'I do love you and I do want to marry you but—'

He held her face in his hands and his eyes were so full of love that she wanted the world to end so that they could be together in another.

'Remember your secret place, darling—the beautiful pool in the jungle where the pilots landed, where hope sprang out of hopelessness? Well, my love is that pool, the eternal hope I'm offering you for the future. We're going home just like those pilots did. We're going to be married and have a family of our own and that's all that matters.'

She clung to him, mouthing kisses across his face, feeling his strength building up her own. 'Is it possible?' she whispered heatedly. 'Oh, I want it to be so very much.'

'Nothing is impossible, darling. Love will see us through. Didn't I promise you you'd be safe with me? Didn't I promise I would never hurt you? I meant it all and I'll keep that promise till the end of time. I love you so very much and I'm taking you home.'

His lips sought hers and she was lost, feeling the intensity of his love and passion in his kiss. He eased her down on the bed and she clung to him as if she would never let him go.

'But not yet,' she murmured as his hands smoothed across her back, urging her into all the delights he could offer—special delights . . . those of passion and love and togetherness.

'No, not yet,' he breathed in her ear. 'Home can wait, your father can wait; "passion with intent" can't.'

'And tomorrow we'll swim with the dolphins and—'

'And make a pilgrimage to our secret place,' he murmured as he eased her pareu down to caress her fiery flesh beneath.

She moved urgently against him, desire and need motivating her hands to claw at his shirt.

'And we ought to go back to the Love Hut and say goodbye and then—'

'Then we might see another secret island and we could be here for a very long time.' He sighed and helped her remove what remained of his clothes. 'And it really doesn't matter how long it takes us to get back but we will . . . eventually.'

'Yes,' she sighed as he moved hungrily across her. 'The world can wait for us, for however long it takes.'

'It might take a long time,' he murmured passionately.

'I love it when we take a long time,' she laughed. And then there was no more laughter, just love and togetherness and the sharing of their passion with delicious intent.

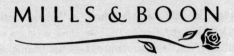

MILLS & BOON

Next Month's Romances

Each month you can choose from a wide variety of romance with Mills & Boon. Below are the new titles to look out for next month.

LAST STOP MARRIAGE	Emma Darcy
RELATIVE SINS	Anne Mather
HUSBAND MATERIAL	Emma Goldrick
A FAULKNER POSSESSION	Margaret Way
UNTAMED LOVER	Sharon Kendrick
A SIMPLE TEXAS WEDDING	Ruth Jean Dale
THE COLORADO COUNTESS	Stephanie Howard
A NIGHT TO REMEMBER	Anne Weale
TO TAME A PROUD HEART	Cathy Williams
SEDUCED BY THE ENEMY	Kathryn Ross
PERFECT CHANCE	Amanda Carpenter
CONFLICT OF HEARTS	Liz Fielding
A PAST TO DENY	Kate Proctor
NO OBJECTIONS	Kate Denton
HEADING FOR TROUBLE!	Linda Miles
WHITE MIDNIGHT	Kathleen O'Brien

MILLS & BOON

Back by Popular Demand

BETTY NEELS

RUBY COLLECTION

A collector's edition of forty favourite titles from one of the world's best-loved romance authors.

Mills & Boon are proud to bring back these sought after titles, now reissued in beautifully matching volumes and presented together in one cherished collection.

Don't miss these unforgettable titles, coming next month:

Title #1   THE DOUBTFUL MARRIAGE
Title #2   A GEM OF A GIRL

Available wherever
Mills & Boon books are sold

Name that Song

How would you like to win a year's supply of simply irresistible romances? Well, you can and they're free! Simply solve the puzzle below and send your completed entry to us by 31st October 1996. The first five correct entries picked after the closing date will each win a years supply of Temptation novels (four books every month—worth over £100).

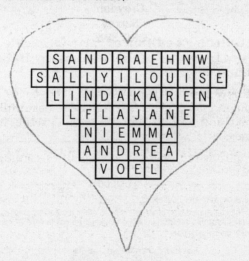

S	A	N	D	R	A	E	H	N	W
S	A	L	L	Y	I	L	O	U	I	S	E
	L	I	N	D	A	K	A	R	E	N
	L	F	L	A	J	A	N	E
	N	I	E	M	M	A
	A	N	D	R	E	A
	V	O	E	L

Please turn over for details of how to enter ☞

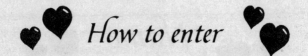 *How to enter*

To solve our puzzle…first circle eight well known girls names hidden in the grid. Then unscramble the remaining letters to reveal the title of a well-known song (five words).

When you have written the song title in the space provided below, don't forget to fill in your name and address, pop this page into an envelope (you don't need a stamp) and post it today! Hurry—competition ends 31st October 1996.

Mills & Boon Song Puzzle
FREEPOST
Croydon
Surrey
CR9 3WZ

Song Title: _____

Are you a Reader Service Subscriber?   Yes ❑   No ❑

Ms/Mrs/Miss/Mr _____

Address _____

_____

_____ Postcode _____

One application per household.

You may be mailed with other offers from other reputable companies as a result of this application. If you would prefer not to receive such offers, please tick box.   ❑

C396
D